Dedic

To all the men and women who die

who paid the ultimate price for independence and those who died on

the maiden voyage.

All have demonstrated immeasurable courage that will continue to

inspire us all.

HM

Prologue

The summer of 1907, Belfast. Antrim's beautiful hills, hidden behind thick industrial smog, fires burning to light the mist rouge, like Hell's kitchen. Fresh air, poisoned by the mills and the shipyards, of metalwork and tobacco factories, the people's temples.

It was a tumultuous time. A time of revolt, a time for inequality. The Irish question.

A ripple, quite un-noticed, echoed through the city like the moan of a siren. The Labour party had arrived for their conference. Hardie, Macdonald and Henderson, British pebbles in an Irish bog. Like wolves, they had left as soon as they had what they wanted, leaving hardly a trace.

Except one stayed behind.

James Larkin had arrived from Glasgow, full of steam to bring Belfast into the modern world of worker's rights. A fair wage for a fair day's work, he decried to the crowds at Speakers Corner, cheers and applause, Michael Riordan was in the crowd. He had been working the shipyards since he was a boy, and in those years, the only change was the ship's name. Ireland was changing for the better, he had hoped.

While Belfast's buildings glowed with lights, the slums grew darker. Catholics were unequal to their Protestant counterparts in all things. Unskilled and disrespected, they were treated as subcontractors for the same work but far less paid, the least in the UK. Backbreaking work as heavy and uncaring as their existence.

The National Union of Dock-labourers, selling ideas of autonomy and a fair wage troubled the factory owners. A fight was coming; even if it were futile, it would show that the working class had a voice to be heard, no matter what the consequences.

Every worker in Belfast stood up to be counted. It was their time. The factory owners, steadfast and secure in their power over their workers, underestimated the people and the power they wielded.

5000 to 10,000 people, every day, attended strike meetings. Riotous protest marches paraded through the city, Catholics and Protestants alike, united this one time for one goal.

Carters, shipyard workers, sailors, firemen, boiler-makers, coal heavers, transport workers, women, children all marched to City Hall to be heard. The Royal Irish Constabulary also went on strike as they were assigned to protect the blackleg workers for no extra pay, much to their families' detriment, it was both a noisy and a silent time. Constable William Barratt refused to protect the blackleg drivers, and he was suspended, which caused an enraged band of brothers to fight for him, and 800 police went on strike.

Both sides had their reasons for striking; an ache went through the city.

The damp, windowless, overcrowded hovels of Sailor-town, the poor riddled with malnutrition, had nothing to lose and were as empty as the union's promises.

The 75 hour week ceased; the factory owners versus the poor, the unassigned, disposable population had the power. Comfortable in the knowledge that this would be over soon, the masses were rising above their station, getting too big for their boots. They needed to be stamped out.

Despite enforcing a compulsory pledge not to join the union, the sackings for joining carried on, which enabled more strikers to join and rebel. There was no end in sight.

No hammers hammered. No mills buzzed. No sirens of the services. Even the military was powerless. Their kin, whom they had to fight in the streets, was torn. Do they fight or do they do nothing, going against one or the other.

It was a cauldron of anger and ire. Of smoke, of heat, of distrust of the owners, the people were an army. Their only weapon was their non-attendance in the factories.

Black-legger's were bought in from Dublin, but they were locked out of the yards and sent back.

The carters went on a sympathy strike refusing to unload goods and transport them to the dock-yards, the 1000 carters who represented the 60 firms also went on strike in sympathy.

Nothing was moving. It was fast becoming a stalemate.

The Catholics, unskilled and subcontracted for piece work, fewer wages and less security, the Protestants, skilled and paid higher even they weren't safe. Women had no financial assistance and were forced back to work, left with no other option.

Belfast saw it's most defining Twelfth. Both Catholics and Protestants came together, the Orange order accompanied, gave rousing speeches in support of the strikers, even Shankhill Road, the volatile road, on the 26th July, 100,000 workers marched to the tune of the Unionist and Nationalist fare. The march rallied to City Hall, joining the other 100,000.

Speeches and rabble-rousing, cheers, and applause echoed, City Hall had to do something. On everyone's lips, Larkin would help us. He would make changes. Our lives would be worth living.

Then it all blew up.

The air thick with fury and vitriol, the crowds gathered, 10,000 strong, this was a summer of do or do not.

All ages and sex, men, women and children all joined in the fight. There were more on strike than as not. The noise, the bellowing of orders to stand down, guns pointed, and the warnings went unheeded, the fight began.

The silence was broken with the crowds' roar, running this way and that, smoke, debris flying through the air hitting anything it came in to contact with. Gunshots, screams, punches, kicks, confusion, fear, a battlefield without a general, and the enemy were too big. The air thick with dust and pellets, breathing nearly impossible, gasping, these were people, not soldiers, trying to obtain their rights, the bloody massacre seemed never-ending.

Shipyard confetti rained down on the army, large rivets, nuts, bolts anything to hand became a weapon. Vans were burned out, buildings attacked, hundreds injured, it was a battlefield in a city that would build the ship of dreams. It was a war zone, and it was out of control. Running through the streets, chaos reigned, the silent factories watched, the machines stood lifeless, redundant.

The strikers became silent as they realised they had been betrayed.

Their demands for a fair wage were dismissed. Scaremongering and playing one off against another, one received more money than the other, lies filtered through the people like the bolts that flew through the air.

Michael ran through the crowds trying to dodge the debris, down he went as an anonymous missile hit him, the pain shooting through his body. Jimmy ran over to help his comrade, shading him from more attacks. Shoulder to shoulder they hobbled to safety, through the smoke bombs and the bullets, they would be the walking wounded that day.

They made it home, the family frantic with worry. They were Catholic, a target. Ma frenzied, blood seeping from his leg, Michael slumped in his chair, Jimmy wiping his brow, Mary stood in shock. What was happening? Had her beloved Ireland come to this?

The night wore on, the fight abated. Like a wounded dog, Michael sat staring. He was close to seeing the creator had Jimmy not saved him.

More desperate talks by Larkin and the factory owners, he had been defeated.

The united became the divided once again. They had failed to get their demands met, but they had made the factory owners realise that the people had power, and they could wield it at any time.

The machines roared back into action, factories became alive again, the union had been formed, and it was a step forward for the dockyard workers and their counterparts, if only very small.

The battle was lost. The scars of the fight remained. Sailor-town, the bone-yard of the fallen, became the prison for the poor.

The unionists bought back like abused wives believing things would get better, forced back into their tired routines.

Ever serving as a reminder that the working class was a dormant army, simmering with injustice and their right to be recognised, bound by the chains of prejudice that would continue on the maiden voyage in April 1912.

Chapter 1

"Oh would you give me a quick kiss Mary, for luck?". Jimmy said, smiling cheekily.

"Get away with ya Jimmy or I'll tell me Da," giggled Mary. It was Sunday afternoon, and Linfield was playing at Belfast Park. The town was rushing with people ready for the match. It was going to be a good one too. Still, it came with its conflict for it was right in the centre of Belfast where both Catholics and Protestants frequented, everyone spoke the language of football, it was the only time they could meet and have something in common, though this treaty would only last 90 minutes.

"Come on Jimmy or we'll be late!" yelled his mate Sean.

"Ok I'm coming, come on Mary, you'll not send me away without a kiss would ya?".

"Ah Jimmy you're a terrible man, here," and she pecked him on the cheek, grinning and rouge with delight.

"You're a good woman Mary. I'll marry you one day you'll see". Jimmy said, giving her a cheeky smile.

"I'll never marry you Jimmy!" she said, laughing and off Jimmy ran into the crowds of flat caps and hobnail boots. A sea of old men, songs, and beer.

As they ran through the streets, they fought their way through the crowds, today was a big match, and they had better hurry. Jimmy had lived in Belfast his entire life and had known Sean since he was wee. They grew up on the same street, fancied the same girls and worked in the same jobs together, they were both labourers, and soon there would be an opportunity neither of them could miss. For it was 1908, and the biggest ship in the world was being built in their home town, it spelled a future for everyone.

The city was awash with people from all over Ireland. Welders, seamstresses, builders, ironworkers, architects, painters.

"Mary, that boys no good, he'll bring ya trouble," said Ma over her sewing.

"Ma give over he's nice, 'sides I've known him since I was a bairn, if it weren't for him we might not have Da with us still after last year. I'm having a tea would like a cup?" asked Mary, trying to change the subject.

"Aye and make one for Da too, no doubt he'll be wanting one, Da you want a cup o tea?" yelled Mary.

A muffled voice shouted through the ceiling something incoherent, but it seemed the answer was no as he was rushing to go out when he appeared.

"Where are you off to then?" asked Ma begrudgingly.

"I'm off to the match with Jimmy. I just heard him I can catch him up," he said breathlessly, rushing to get his boots on.

"Does he know you're going with him? He didn't seem like he did, anyway, since when do you go to the football?" asked Ma sarcastically.

"I can go if I want," he replied defiantly.

"You can go if you want. You want drinking more like".

Mary smiled as she poured the tea. Her mom and dad were from the old times. It's true, like any Irish man, her dad did like a drink. It'd be a sin not to really.

"Oh well you be careful, there are fights breaking out all over the city lately, you just stay with Jimmy ok".

"Argh, I'm not a child Ma, I'll be fine, I gotta go, or I'll never catch him up". Ma was fussing over him like a child, tying his scarf and buttoning his coat.

"That man, 20 years we've been married, and I still worry about him like he was me own flesh and blood. Where's that tea?".

Ma was right. There were murders and fights happening all over the city. Sinn Fein was still young and they were vehemently against Home Rule. It was Ireland for the Irish at any cost.

Sectarianism was rising and if anyone got in the way, they didn't get in the way for very long.

"We will put up a grand fight, a right to save the Soul of Ireland", yelled Tom Clarke, he was the leader of the Irish Republican Brotherhood. His words touched every Irish man and woman. He irked the English. He was being watched as was his group.

Standing on a box at Speakers Corner, surrounded by like-minded others.

"There will be a grand fight, and that fight will save the soul of Ireland! The next blow for Irish freedom, have no doubt, Ireland will strike, will win through, we die happy!" he decried with passion.

The crowd cheered and applauded. His eyes scanning making sure he met with everyone,

"If you strike at, imprison, or kill us, out of our prisons or graves, we still evoke a spirit that will thwart you, and raise a force that will destroy you! We defy you! Do your worst! Now is the time, our time, time to fight, for we fight for our future, the future of Ireland!" he declared.

As he shouted these words, surrounded by crowds, football fans sailed by, it was a shame that this rousing speech was today of all days, it was a big match and football was a language everyone spoke. "Jimmy hold up," puffed Michael, pushing through the crowds.

"Michael, what you doing 'ere?" laughed Jimmy surprised to see him.

"I thought I'd join ya, wet me whistle".

"How you doing there Mr Riordan, Mrs Riordan ok is she?" beamed Sean.

"Oh she's ok, she taking tea at home".

Jimmy was smiling.

"Come on or we'll never get there".

They waded through the crowds, passed Tom and his soapbox, his words echoing over the noise, the pub, The Dockers Rest, like a beacon loomed over them, it's welcoming scent of stale beer and a tuneless piano playing, the ale flowing freely.

A man flew through the doors with the help of two burly looking men, women jigged on tables, men desperately held their beer lest they spill a drop, a mist of pipe smoke filled the air and the lights glistened through the glasses above the bar.

"Oh Jaysus we'll miss half the match we'll ne' r get served", cried Michael.

"Aye we will, three of ya best there lovely" waved Sean. He was a tall chap with a glint in his eye, he could charm the pants off the ladies that one. He was nice with it, whoever he spoke to, usually the ladies, once they saw his clear blue eyes that was it, they were his, his smile was contagious and he always got what he wanted. His wispy brown hair, he was the tallest in his family, his Ma said that she left him under the mulberry bush too long, his Da said he was the height of the milkman, he was definitely his dad's son though, they had the same eyes, the same gift of the gab.

They struggled through the bar and went to the match. Neither were

separated for your beliefs so fights were always breaking out.

They shuffled through to the bleacher's, the drums and the slurs were

a cacophony. Today was the final of the Ulster championships.

Hidden guns and fighting paraphernalia in abundance, danger lurked.

"Come on ya bastards", shouted some.

"Get it up ye" yelled another. To some, it was a bit of fun, to others,

it was deep down hatred.

The beer swished and the smoke rose from the old men and their

moustaches, one beer turned in to three and out came the teams.

Antrim versus Cavan. The crowds cheered, and they kicked off.

Ninety minutes later, it was all over. 3-0 to Antrim.

They all filed out the stadium, a sea of brown suits and flat caps.

"Oh what a load, did you see that ref? It was a fixed game, we never

had a chance", whined one.

"Me Ma could have kicked better", chirped another.

Their woes were made better with liquid gold and the three

sauntered home. As they walked passed the old shops, posters had

been put up advertising jobs coming to the cities docks.

"Wanted: skilled labourers to build the world's biggest ship. Fair wages paid. Meet at Queens Island 6 am Harland and Wolff", read Sean.

"What's that then? Worlds biggest ship, won't be for the likes of us", said Jimmy.

"Is it ever for us? We build it, but that's as close as we'll get, sounds good though, you gonna apply Michael? Weren't you a welder before?".

"Aye, I was the best", he lamented.

"I'll go with ya", laughed Jimmy.

"You've never welded in a ya life".

"How hard could it be? I'm strong, you could teach me".

"Teach you?" laughed Michael, "Aye, I guess I could, and what about you there Sean, would you be with us if you can tear yourself away from the ladies?".

"I'll think about it".

"You'll think about it? Why? Do you have urgent business to attend? You'll think about it, you'll apply for sure ya will, ya Mam could do with the housekeeping" scolded Michael, they were good lads, but Sean was the joke of the trio, he was a good worker, Jimmy was a labourer and Michael was a jack of all trades. The riots the previous year caused him pain; he was standing in the wrong place when the metal reigned down from the sky. He was lucky to be alive. He was amongst the hundreds who were starving and impoverished, and he desperately needed money, and beer doesn't pay for itself.

The next day the trio went to the dock to sign up for work. In a world where the working class was seen as lazy and workshy, the army of men that roamed the streets looking for work put this to bed. The crowds of men all jostling like show ponies while the foreman took his pick. He needed skill and reliability, he had his personal reasons why he didn't pick you, it was not always obvious and it was an unfair competition. But, it was his choice, and though difficult, decisions had to be made, he had to make sure his were correct. Each man desperate for work, they all had poverty in common.

You could have a job today, and tomorrow you'd be back to begging. Since the strike last year, things hadn't gotten much better. Catholic against Protestant in all things, even begging.

The foreman, Mr Kingan, as he was known, was a formidable no-nonsense man. Walking the lines with his hands in his braces, examining the crowds like one does when picking good olives. Some were bad, some were good. Some had missing limbs from previous work; others were too young, others too weak. The sound was deafening. It was a cattle market.

"Good morning everybody", he bellowed like a schoolmaster. "I need strong workers, reliable, I'll take no slackers, it's dirty work, long hours but it's a fair wage, and you'll find nowt else in this city. You lad", pointing at Jimmy, "what do they call ya?".

"Jimmy, they call me Jimmy".

"Jimmy? What do you do?".

"I'm a labourer, best in Belfast," he said with a cheeky grin.

Mr Kingan looked him up and down like he was an annoying insect and moved on, "What do you do?" to Michael.

"I'm a welder sir, Jimmy's me mate and Sean here, in Belfast, we're hard workers you'll see".

"Yes, I'm sure I will, ok, you three come on," and he wandered off, interrogating more men and picking them out the crowd. Once he had chosen his bunch, the rest sauntered off, they would try again the next day as the work was ongoing and this ritual was a display of power for Mr Kingan, he had people to answer to, and on his head it fell if the workers failed to keep up.

The lads followed to the slipway 3, the home of ship 401, the giant towers of metal, looming over the sea, their height intimidating. Metal gantry's 228 feet high and could be seen from the city. Six thousand tons of steel, noise equal to any battlefield, it was a domineering sight. Thousands of people flooded the area, being watched over by the ship's architect Thomas Andrews.

Lines of desperate men waiting to be assigned work drew the eye. Like a military exercise, the men were then picked again and divided up. Greeting them all was a little man in a window.

"Sign here. This is your time board, you'll need it to clock in and out or you'll not get paid. You can bring your own tools, you break or lose your tools, that's your problem, watch them like a hawk there's tea leaves around here. You're late for work that's a five-shilling fine, you get seven minutes break a day, and it's six am until six pm and Saturday eight until four, so if you have a drink on Friday don't even think about calling in sick. You get Sundays off, to pray for ya sins, I'm sure you'll have enough time for that. The work is hard and long, I need teams of five. At least one of you must be left-handed. I need young lads too, Jack'll show you around", reeled off the man in the office.

Sean, Jimmy, Michael, and two young lads who wouldn't see their 16th birthday followed Jack to the dock.

The air was shattered like stained glass as hammers against metal clashed in an eternal discord. The noise would make the Somme sound like a quiet afternoon.

The lads followed Jack, the heat of the ironworks, the smoke, it was a city in a city, men running this way and that. Everything had to be precise. There was no room for error.

Examining the gang, Jack asked, "Lads, what are you called?".

The two young ones answered, "Sam, James".

"Right Sam, you'll be the catch boy, James you'll be the heater boy, this fire needs to be kept lit and hot at all times, so it's your responsibility to keep things going, you heat up the rivets, throw these things to Sam who will then pass it to you", pointing at Jimmy. Pieces of metal resembling foolishly large nails were to be hammered into the ship, like a sewing kit to keep it all together. Plates upon plates of metal, time was a factor as the metal cools very quickly, it was dangerous even for the most skilled.

Sam was given his leather glove to carry the rivets. There were no replacements if it was damaged or lost. Carrying from the furnace to placing it in the plates took less than one minute. Any shoddy work would be spotted by the rivet counter and docked from your pay, and you'd have to redo it and pay for the materials as well. Ship-work was not a job for those that wanted to make money easily.

"Jimmy, are ya left or right-handed?" asked Jack.

"Right".

"You? Are ya left or right-handed?" glaring at Michael.

"Oh, I be left-handed, me mother said I was born on the devil's side," he smiled cheekily.

Shaking his head, Jack replied, "I don't care about where you born ya eejit, you two will be hitting this in that metal panel, as it cools it'll fit, it's hard work, and there are millions that need to be done, as you can see it's fairly high up so no messing, it's dangerous, and I don't have the time to scrape yers off the floor, if you don't know how to do something the lads will help ye, this is where you'll work, the more rivets you do, the more you get paid, it's one and a half penny per rivet. The rivet counter comes by on a Saturday, so if you're doing it wrong, you get docked, they're tight bastards, there's no arguing, no debate, so do it right, get it!".

The lads murmured as if they were being scolded by the headmaster. They knew their place in the world was the bottom of a great pit with slippery sides.

"Nearly all the men are mutton so you'll either need to shout or learn the Morse code, though you'll be too busy working for that".

"Morse code?! Sure where do we learn that, Morse code, tap-tapping away, how could they hear it through the noise?" laughed Sean looking to the others for reassurance.

"You'll pick it up quicker than you think young lad, any of these can learn it I'm sure a simple one like yourself can". This met with an evil look and private smiles from his comrades.

The banging of the hammers on metal seemed louder, whether it was a secret message or the insertion of the rivets was anyone's guess at this point. The clanging, the heat, the eternal noise, it was never-ending, a long drawn out cacophony, it made the body vibrate to the point of shell shock.

As Jack pointed up, they were like tiny flies with giant creatures ready to squash them. Eighty feet above them were the stages. This is where they would stand and work on the massive metal panels. The panels were 30 feet high and 6 feet across, some required double rivets, and if you had a weak composition, one dizzy spell, over you go, as many forgotten workers did.

"If any of you have your own tools on your head be it, you lose it, it's your problem not ours, there's a lot of thieves about, bloody Catholics, can't trust none of em".

Catholics still were the runts of the litter in Belfast. They were treated terribly, given the most dangerous, dirty jobs and were the blame for the ills of the Irish.

Their lot in life was worse than the worst. They were subject to violence, banishment and ridicule. They shared Sailor-town with the Protestants. Sailor-town was the centre of the dockyard workers' homes if you can call it that. Only last year, the riots and strikes ran through it, transients came and went, and so stood the buildings, the squalid doss houses, always watching, always ready to take dwellers desperate for any sort of roots. The families would come from one damp, flea-infested rat hole to another, but the houses remained, ready to consume the next. And so it went on. Sailor-town was not a place that could be called romantic if the infections didn't get you, the criminals would. And for the poor Catholics, the criminals would sniff them out; fights were in abundance, and justice was as scarce as a hot meal and comfortable bed.

"We're supposed to work up there?" said Jimmy incredulously, looking up, hiding his eyes from the sun.

"Well yeah, how else dya think we gonna build it? Not all ships come in bottles ya know," said Jack laughing.

"We be closer to God up there, Jaysus, well how do we get up there?" asked James.

"Oh very special, we all em ladders, wooden tings you climb em".

"Aw ya a funny one ain't ya".

"Not scared of heights are ya boy?".

"Me, nah, I ain't scared of notin, just the highest thing I ever saw," said James. It was true. She was a tall structure, seen for miles. It was a big drop for the passengers who would leap off her soon.

"Well it's unny high when you're down here, when you're up there, down here looks even more so, so be careful, we already lost a few men this week pissing about, you're the replacements and I don't want to have to keep showing new people the same shite every day, see how long ya last". A silence diminished the laughter.

"Ya lost men? What do you mean, what happened?" asked Sean.

"Name was Robert, just started with us, up there he was, fell off the staging, his son works on the other ship, the Olympic over there, nasty business so be careful, one eye open at all times, left a wife and five kids".

The men all became too aware of the work they were to embark on, the ship of dreams was fast becoming a mausoleum, built in death before she even sailed.

"I expect hard work and don't go doing any home jobs, you work on the ship and notin else ya get me! If ya get caught, it's straight to Crumlin. Everything is logged so anything missing or shoved up ya shirts, on your head be it".

Though it was Harland and Wolff, it was also a community of thieves, gamblers and jokers. All sorts went on under the noses of the overseers. They knew it happened, but what could they do, sack the whole workforce? They were discreet and it was a tidy mini-industry within an industry where a few bob could be made for the right man.

"When do we start then?" asked Michael.

"Come tomorrow morning 6 am sharp, breakfast is at 8:30 am so don't forget ya piece, James you be here a half-hour early to get the furnaces started, you don't turn up or you're late you'll be for it, not just by me but by your team, that fire doesn't get lit and heated you won't be able to make the rivets, no rivets no pay so get your lazy arse in".

"Ok, I will," murmured James, he was 14, and his meagre pay would help his Ma and Da immensely. There was no real schooling, and at that age, you were a man, he drank and smoked like his Da, he was a hard worker and looked well beyond his small years.

He was a small boy, meek-looking, but he was strong and had the mind of a much older man, children weren't children then, there were no toys, no fun, no ambition, if he didn't work there's a chance they could lose their lodgings despite how grim they were, it was better than being on the streets or worse, the workhouse.

The lads left. The final words, about Robert, were ringing in their ears to the din of the noise.

It was a dangerous job, with great risk, but they had little choice. As they walked away, the idle wind from the sea ran around them. The temperature dropped the further away from the dockyard they got; it was hot at Hell's fire. It was like an open mine, men slaving away, every day could be their last day, one slip and they would be a memory—an entry into the history of ship 401.

Chapter 2

"Come on there Michael, would ya hurry up we be late for the first day" shouted Jimmy from the street.

"I'm just getting me cap!" a yell through the door.

"Jimmy, you working up at the docks? I didn't know you were a seamstress," laughed Mary.

"Ah ya a funny one Mary. I'm going to be the riveter on the world's biggest ship", replied Jimmy leaning on the door, smiling at her.

"Sure what do you know about riveting? The only thing you work is ya tongue".

"Gimme a little kiss and I'll show ya what me tongue can do," he laughed.

"Ohh Jimmy ya dirty scoundrel away wi ya," Mary replied, flicking a tea towel at him. Ma, making tea, gave a private smile to herself. She remembered when she was a lass and Michael was a terrible flirt too.

"Mary, are you going down there too? They have seamstress jobs too, I'm sure".

"Are you looking out for me, Jimmy?".

"Of course, you're me girl".

"Your girl? Is that right? You best put a ring on me finger or I'll be snapped up".

"Who be wanting to snap you up Mary, it's in the stars, you're all mine".

"Oh I can hardly wait, besides, yes, I am a seamstress. I start today with Milly, making lace for the ship, the best seamstress in Belfast".

"The best? Well, Mary, you'll be able to afford your own ring then, ya can buy me one too," joked Jimmy.

"Enough of your chat, you'll be late before you've started, away with you, Da don't forget your piece and don't eat it all at once, there be notin else until ya get home" shouted Ma.

"I won't, Ma, what we having today?" asked Michael examining the contents.

"Today, my love, it's leftover cabbage on ya bread".

"Oh Ma cabbage again, Jaysus, if I ever taste another cabbage," he cried.

"Well starve then, ungrateful beggar," she tutted. Food was as and when, there was not much choice, and meat was once a week if they could afford it. There were worse foods.

"See ya later, Ma," and he rushed out the door.

The old buildings, soaring reminders of Victorian Britain, looked down on them as they ran to the docks, black squads of men of all ages, even the catch boys with their little hands, what they lacked in education they made up for in spirit. Mary was sat with her mother by the fire. Outside was dreary and noiseless. They didn't have much, but what they had they were grateful for.

"Da, he hasn't worked in a while ya think he be ok?" she asked.

"He'll be fine, strong as an ox, besides it'll get him from under me feet, and we need the money, finest ship in the world they say".

"Not that we'll be able to go on it," scorned Mary. She was a strong-willed, young lass, and times were changing for everyone.

"Now Mary, you know that's not for like the of us, sure the union says they help the workers but not the women, and certainly not for travel tickets. Aye, last year with the riots, we were lucky to be alive, oh what a mess that was, and for what? Union, bah, may as well be a bunch of scarecrows all the good they do, and where is that Larkin fella now, probably rustling up some more trouble that one".

Ma was indignant of the last year's riots, she was right, there were no gains and only losses, Michael got injured in the clashes, and he was lucky to be alive. Mary had his fire in her belly but was castrated by society. She could no more change her station than stop the tide from coming in.

The lads, walking through the city to the dockyard was a mass of people. Time was getting on, and they had to hurry.

The shipyard, a crowd of men all signing in to get their time boards, and walking to the stages, James, with his face already blackened by the heat of the furnace was ready for the gang, Sam, went to his station and awaited the first rivet, Sean waited for the catch boy and Jimmy and Michael were waiting for Sean. They didn't have to wait long.

James removed the rivet from the brazier, and the heat was like a thousand suns. He rolled it along with the metal plate to Sam, who then caught it in his leather mitt.

Sean, on his heels, took the rivet from Sam and inserted it into the hole where Michael and Jimmy were working, and they bashed it like there was no tomorrow.

"Come on, Michael, harder!" shouted Jimmy.

"I'm going as best I can, son, come on ya bastard!" as he hammered it into place.

Sean pushing the other side to keep it in, it was a job not for the weak, it was a hot and dirty place like the bowels of hell.

Once in, a new one arrived, and so it was for 12 hours a day, rivet after rivet, hundreds of men, no respite from the thunderous clash of metal on metal.

"Jaysus Christ, I'm bloody knackered," wheezed Jimmy.

Michael laughed. It was back-breaking work and for all its hardships, it was rewarding. You worked hard and though the pay was not much, you felt a sense of achievement.

"Coming through!!" yelled Sean through the metal plate, the red hot rivet glowing it's face at them, red with fury as it was bashed over and over to get it in place. Mocking them to hit harder and faster.

"God, I'm bloody dying here, I need a drink," said Jimmy wiping his brow.

"Well, ya ain't bloody getting one till breakfast, or ya wanna waste your seven minutes," laughed Sean.

"I'm getting a brew, pass me that can over there, hey lad come 'ere" bellowed Michael from up high, a young lad below looked up. Even though he was way below, he was still small in stature.

"Fill this up would ya I'm parched".

"No way, I get me hide tanned if I get caught," shouted the lad.

"Don't get caught then. There's a penny in it for ya".

"Show me the penny!" he yelled up.

"Show you the penny, argh ya cheeky sod here, and hurry up it's hotter than a barmaids promise up here".

Michael lowered the can with the penny slowly, crosswinds threatening to take it as it swung. The lad grabbed the can and took the penny.

"He's gonna rob ya Michael, ya'll have no tea and lose a penny," laughed Jimmy.

"If he robs me, I'll launch this hammer at him," he laughed.

"Then you'll lose more money for lost tools," laughed Jimmy.

"Come on, will ya get working, soon be breakfast anyway," shouted Sean.

The little lad ran and was gone for what seemed like eons and surprisingly came back with a steaming can of what Michael hoped was tea. Reeling it up, the steam met his blackened face, drinking from the can it was as if it was sent by the Gods themselves. The brown nectar touching his lips, the sweet taste of sugar, rejuvenated him and the lads, this time, no one saw. He might not be so lucky next time. A minor thing as having a cuppa was the same as stealing. You were on Harland and Wolff time, not your own. You were paid to work, not to drink tea.

The morning wore on, and sunlight was shining through massive clouds. The thunderous clanging disappeared in their heads as they worked, only audible to visitors and the new.

Here and there, welders, invisible to the naked eye covered in black grime and grease, were identified by sporadic white flashes of welding irons and the orange sparkle of metal raining down to the joiners below. Welders flashes caused immense headaches and could render you out of work for days, they, like everyone else, were replaceable and carried on regardless in this grim husk of a ship.

Thousands of men all doing the same thing, gangs of men and boys, crunched up into the smallest places with only a hammer in hand and a thin piece of wood between them and oblivion.

One ran the risk of injury at all times. No matter how careful you were, planks of wood would fall from higher levels with devastating consequences, burns, breaks. You could even lose your head if you stepped in the wrong place.

These men were warriors. They were as strong as the ship. They too, were built in iron and steel.

The team hammered away at the rivets, Sam and James, aged heavily with their work, ached at the morning's work. The air was muggy with smoke and heat, breathing was hard, and everyone smoked. It was cheaper to smoke than to eat, and smokes could be used as currency.

Jack walked about his kingdom, keeping an eye on the new workers.

"Look, it's that Jack, coming to check on us, quick hide that can or you'll be for it," scorned Jimmy.

"Looks he's checking the rivets, cheeky bastard, don't see him sweating his bollocks off hitting this".

Jack walked over to them with an accusing eye.

"Morning lads, how you doing today, working hard, I hope, let's see what you're doing".

They moved out the way as Jack stroked the cool rivets, checking the plates were in the right place and no shirking. He looked at the lads and gave an intake of breath.

"Very good work lads, very good, how many of these have you done so far?".

"About 25", said Sean proudly.

"25! In an hour!? You need to do more than that I have lads down there doing twice that much in the least time, lazy bastards, get back to work, I want 30 more by breakfast, or I'll dock ya a shilling for everyone you don't get in, I'll be watching you, all of you, best be 30 done you got half an hour, get to it" exclaimed Jack to scornful looks.

"30! Is he mad? I'm already working like a Trojan," puffed Michael.

"Less of your moaning come on, Sam, hurry the feck up would ya Christ's sake," shouted Jimmy.

"Don't blaspheme Jimmy, oh the lord be watching," Michael said, crossing himself in penance.

"The Lord be watching my arse, I'll be with him soon enough if I work any harder, come on Sam!" yelled Jimmy, he couldn't afford to lose this job if he wanted to marry Mary. Michael loved Jimmy like a son, and he could do no wrong, he was a good man, a dedicated man. The son he never had.

Sam came running, rivet in hand and Sean took it the lads bashed it and bashed it as if it was Jacks face staring at them, one after the other after the other, sweat pouring like rain, poor Sam running this way and back again with more rivets and James desperately keeping the fire going. It was a production line of exhausted faces and molten steel, hearts were pumping as fast as the pumps would in the Atlantic, let's hope these ones lasted longer.

Jack appeared up the plank to them, secure that they would fail, and he could wield his power to both humiliate and control them. He hated their cockiness and was sure they would be out on their arse. "So girls, hope you didn't break a nail with the work, move out the way, let me look," as he pushed Michael out the way. He knelt down, examining the work looking for faults, the petty man looked close. Running his hands over the rivets.

"We done over 30 sir", asserted Sean.

Jack was disappointed. The rivets were perfect. He stood up and stared at them all. In silence, he turned and left. They had won this round. A wave of breath left the lads, the first morning done.

The bell rang, and salvation came. It was 8:30 and breakfast time.

Chapter 3

The men all sat back wiping their sodden foreheads of sweat and grime, beads of black gems running down battered faces and grey shirts.

The rush to the hot water boilers was fierce. Pushing and jostling in the little time they had. Greasy fingers and all manner of vessels to carry hot water and tea clamoured. Michael pushed through the crowd to get to the taps. There was no politeness about this. Unbeknownst to them, the gaffers were walking about assessing the masses. Walking proudly and the crowds parting like the red sea.

"Who's that?" Jimmy asked an equally grim looking welder.

"They're the hats, top brass, they make sure we stay in line, bunch of pricks never lift a finger. They were one of us once, but they moved up now they think they're summat special. Stick a hat on him thinks he's God".

"Yeah, God of pricks" spoke another.

"Oh they got someone". A hush went through the crowd, one eye on the hats and one on the can being filled.

"Got someone? What you mean 'they got someone'?" asked Jimmy.

"Shush watch, if they catch ya doing anything but work they'll have ya, they have no qualms about giving ya the belt if you look at them wrong".

The hat, second rung down from management kept the yard going. They had more power than Jack who also answered to them, only they could make him tremor. They could sack you just like that, but that wasn't their way. Their way was to bully and coerce and look out for even the most minor infraction. They were the scabs of the strikes, never believed in unions, and the men were cattle that could be chastised and handled how they saw fit. All eyes were on them. Three of them stood around a youngish lad, not very old and not very sharp either. Kevin Dunleavy. A simple but hard-working lad had left a few minutes early to beat the rush of the crowds to the watering benches. In his defence, he did it so he could go back to work earlier and carry on, though a good reason, freedom of thought was not permitted. He stood there, terrified like a child. Head down, arms at his sides. His stature was of a sorry dog though his build, he could easily cause some physical damage should he get the confidence to do it. He was sweet-natured and trusting, but in a shipyard, he was seen as an easy target, weak, malleable, a fool.

They circled him like wolves. Prickles on his forehead manifested through fear. Had his bladder not just been emptied, he would have done it there and then.

"What's your name, boy?" asked one.

Looking at his feet, "Kevin," he murmured.

"What? Boy speak up", he authoritatively.

"Kevin, sir".

"Kevin, sir", laughed one mocking him.

"Who's that one, the one talking?" asked Jimmy.

"Oh he's the worst, Mr Bourne, evil bastard, don't wanna be messing with him".

"Mr Bourne, is he allowed to do that?".

"He can do what he likes, or you can get another job".

The chastising continued.

"How is it that you have your can ready and filled and the horn only just got started? Mr Quint, what time did you ring that horn?".

"830am on the dot Mr Bourne, never late with it neither".

"On the dot you say, so Kevin either you're a marathon runner, or Mr Quint's watch is out, which is it?".

"I don't know, sir". He could feel red in his face with fear and embarrassment. Mr Bourne's eyes were drilling into him.

"What? Speak up, lad, what's wrong with you? I wager you left that stage early to get your tea quicker than these hard-working folk, are you better than them boy? Do you get special treatment, are you a prince, look at me boy". Bourne said, sternly grabbing his shirt and pulling him up, so he looks at him eye to eye. Jimmy jumped to his rescue but was pulled back by the others.

"Don't! You don't want him to notice you, leave it he can take care of himself".

"Sir, I only meant to do it earlier so I could go back to work earlier. I'm sorry," he cried.

"Keen aren't ya? Are you a simpleton boy? What's wrong with you? Docile? Give me that can," and he snatched it off him. Pouring away the contents.

"Little shit, get back to work, your breaks over and I'm docking ya as well. There now you can get back to work early as you wanted".

Kevin was downhearted and sniffed as he walked away. An atmosphere of anger and revenge was brewing amongst the brothers. This would not do.

As the three walked through the crowds laughing, Kevin sauntered up the gangplank to his station. He was a child in a man's body and this would be his life. He was simple in his mind. He worked as hard as everyone else and never shirked responsibility, but he couldn't stand up for himself. His 5 foot 4 stocky frame could take even the hardest of men, but he had a gentle temperament and wouldn't even hurt a fly.

Jimmy watched him walk up the plank. Thoughts of revenge running through his mind.

"Who does he think he is, needs teaching a lesson he does".

"Yeah, he does," said another.

Telling glances of concurring thoughts ran through. Mr Bourne would get his comeuppance.

Chapter 4

The day wore on at the dock. The earlier fracas still on every man's mind. They were a brotherhood and looked out for each other. Meanwhile, in the city, the heavy atmosphere was spreading. Tom Clarke was holding a meeting of minds. English Rule was something they all agreed must end, and the only way was to fight. They were done with the talking. It was time for firepower.

Chapter 5

"They oughtn't to get away with it, Da it's bullying," hissed Jimmy.

"It's none of our business Jimmy, get on with the hammering, or we'll be for it again, we're on his radar, you watch he'll be checking on us every chance he gets" panted Michael as he hit the rivet.

The iron rivet protested it's position to the bitter end, in it went like steel cattle herded into a plate.

Below them, the same conversation was being had. Everyone wanted to get Bourne. He was a pitiless man, he had too much power and loved his job. He walked around like it was his yard, safe that he was untouchable. Jobs were scarce, and no one would stand up to him, fear kept the men in line. For now.

Hours would pass with hard work, there were no clocks, the poor did not need a pocket watch as they had nowhere else to be.

Hammers and a blazing fire roared on, the muscles of the arm getting tired at the hammering and the pushing, the forges working to capacity to produce the massive plates for the sides of the ship. Six feet by 30ft, these colossal plates transported around the dock on trains that wouldn't see you through the smoke, so you had to be careful not to get in the way.

Cranes above arched their necks carrying girders and all sorts of metal to the slipway, dominating the Belfast skyline.

Giants on the horizon were watching over the city like angry Gods. Flat caps and flannel shirts, canvas shoes, there was no work attire, and you couldn't just go to the shop for replacements. It was a mend and make do society. The homes the men lived in had no indoor toilets, so sharing a street with hundreds of families and six kids in each, all hungry, all dirty, there was no way to keep clean.

The air was contaminated with dust, and the smell of smoke and oil filled the air. It was a desolate, dark place with no end.

Their first day was over. Twelve hours of hammering and grinding, the weary workhorses returned home. The spirit and excitement of the morning had been sucked out of them and beaten into submission. It would go on like this for three million more rivets.

Jimmy gathered his things and walked down the plank with his crew.

As he did, he noticed one of the crowd from earlier waiting for him.

He wanted a word in private.

"Hey, what's up," asked Jimmy.

"Come on, we having a meeting, about earlier," he said sheepishly.

"Jimmy, are ya coming?" shouted Michael.

"I'll catch yers up, Da, carry on," waved Jimmy.

They walked around the side of the building, and awaiting them

were two others. Trying to remain calm, Jimmy followed.

"Lads, what's happening?".

"Who's this?" said one.

"Jimmy, he's new, I'm Andy, that's Colin, that's No Nose" to subtle

nods.

"No nose? Sure why you call him that?" said Jimmy laughing.

"Cause if you ask him anything he knows notin, he'll never rat ya

out," said Colin.

"Oh, ok, so what we doin?".

"That thing earlier, Bourne, we gonna get him are yers in?" asked

Andy between puffs of a cigarette. No Nose was watching on.

"In? In what? Ya can't do anytin or you'll end up in Crumlin".

"Only if ya get caught".

"And you jokers won't get caught? Thanks I'm out". Jimmy turned to go.

Andy took his arm, "wait now, listen, we just need you to keep a lookout for Bourne, if you see him, drop a bolt down to me, and I'll do the rest, we work under yers".

"And what you gonna do, morder him? Get away withja," and he started to walk away.

"We just gonna show him it's not right what he did to Kev, he's gotta go".

"Go? Go where?".

"You leave that to us, the less you know, the better,"

"But I know the same now as I did then, I'm off, see yers tomorrow," and off he scarpered to meet Michael. They were waiting by the gate for him. Floods of blackened men, a river of shadows along the streets to Sailor-town, made their way from one grimy prison to another.

"What was all that about Jimmy?" asked Sean,

"I don't know but tomorrow something's happening".

"Is it to do with that Kevin fella, argh ya best not get mixed up with that for sure, you'll cop it knowing your luck," claimed Michael.

"No I'm not doing notin, come on, I'm starving, stomach feels like me throats been cut".

The horde of workers swamped the streets. Some went to the bars, some went home. Most lived on the same street and almost everyone was related through in-laws, cousins, second cousins.

Nothing was secret and if it was, it wasn't for long. There were codes and words that only a select few would know. Ears were everywhere. Though most of them were deaf from the riveting.

Mary and Ma were busying themselves to get the tea ready, Ma having made the best she could out of what she could afford, cabbage stew, Da wouldn't be happy but he was starving and when you're hungry you'll eat anything. Now the money was coming in, they could hopefully afford to eat better.

"Do you tink Da be ok down there, it's a long day," asked Mary.

"Don't you worry, he's made of strong stuff your Da, you take after him, strong-willed," said Ma as she laid the wooden table. It was passed down through the families. New things were a rare thing, and if it were new, she wouldn't use it. Except if the priest came down. He always turned up when it was time for tea, he'd eat all he could, preach a little and leave. Mary didn't understand why he didn't just buy the food himself it seems that's all he wanted.

"Now Mary what a thing to say, Father Patterson is the best priest we ever had around here, I could listen to his sermons forever".

"As long as he can stop eating our biscuits for long enough".

"Mary shame on you," said Ma crossing herself.

"Well, he does, I thought gluttony was a sin".

"He works very hard for the community".

"I bet he doesn't do 12 hour days for a few bob".

"Mary, I won't have you talk like that in this house, tomorrow you'll go and confess what you just said, oh my lord".

"Oh Ma," as Mary was about to go on her rants about the working class in walked the trio. Black faces only noticeable for the whites of their eyes. Dust and debris falling from them as they gathered in from the night. If it weren't for the street lamps, they wouldn't have been seen at all.

They announced their arrival, coughing up all the gunk they had breathed in all day.

You worked until you died, there was no recompense, nothing to help when you couldn't breathe and who could afford a doctor anyway?

A whirlwind of black dust filled the room, infecting everything it touched. Making the small room even smaller and darker.

Michael headed for his chair by the fire and gave a long sigh. The chair was his throne, it was heaven just to sit down and do nothing if only for a few minutes.

His sigh belied his age, for a man of forty-five, he looked a man twice his age. His lungs weren't strong and his body matched. Ma looked at him sympathetically. Mary busied herself. It was hard to look at her dad like this. He was her world, the rock she depended on, his work fuelled her anger to the factory and dockyard owners.

She joined the strikers the previous year too, but had stayed home when the riot happened much to her chagrin. Her mother forbade her to go out for fear she would be imprisoned or killed. As much as Mary had strength in her voice.

Chapter 6

"Ah Mary get us a cup of tea wouldja, us working men are thirsty".

"Good lord, look at you three, sure I wouldn't recognise ya,"

exclaimed Ma, fiercely batting away the dust out the back door.

Hats came off and boots left at the door, hands by the fire. Tea was

predictably laid out, a smell of cabbage stew engulfed the tiny room.

Their legs weighed a ton and could hardly lift their arms to sup the

tea. Sean hovered by Mary.

They discussed the day and the goings-on but omitted the story

about poor Kevin Dunleavy.

"Oh Mary, rub me feet I had a day and a half" laughed Jimmy.

"I wouldn't touch your feet if my loife depended on it, you're black

as the ace of spades,

shouldn't you be getting home, won't ya mammy have your tea

ready?".

"How can I eat dere when I have such a beautiful woman to look

after me 'ere".

"Get on withja, I'm laying me dads tea, Sean would ya get out me way you're worse than a cat under me feet" tutted Mary as bought over the pot of stew.

"Sorry Mary, How are ye Mary, nice to see yersel, listen your friend Milly, is she er working at the factory as well?" said Sean coyley. Suspiciously Mary answered, "Why yes she is tomorrow, with me, why?".

"Ah no reason, just making conversation". Sean was never bashful around the girls except Milly.

With Milly, he was shy, courteous, it was sweet. He had known her since he was a boy, they all went to school together. Jimmy had his football and Sean secretly harboured feelings for her, watching from afar. Milly had known about how he felt but she also hid her feelings. Her father wouldn't haven't liked it his daughter going with boys, it would be a one-way ticket to the Magdalene laundries if she stepped out of line.

Mary smiled, it was an open secret that they liked each other but they never really spoke, maybe he was getting more confident with the idea now he was growing up.

She may see him as a man now instead of the frightened boy who used to run from her in the street.

"Would you like me to pass her a message Sean? You might see her in the morning. The factory isn't too far from where you are," Mary said helpfully.

"Oh nah, it's ok. It's nothing really, just being polite". Sean was a tall lad, his wavy brown hair and blue eyes, he knew how handsome he was, the girls would come running to him,

but his heart belonged to Milly.

"I'll be seeing you tomorrow Jimmy, me Ma be wondering where I am".

"See you tomorrow Sean lad, Mary I'm off then if ya not gonna rub me feet".

Sean disappeared out the door with Jimmy, Mary gave a smile to herself.

Chapter 7

The next morning Mary was walking with Milly, bursting to tell her about Sean. It was a warm day, the sun was shining and workers milled on the way to work.

"So Milly, I know someone who likes you," said Mary smiling.

Frowning, Milly gave a puzzled look. "Likes me? Sure who would that be?".

"Oh he's a dear friend of ours, he's single he's very nice".

"Oh God Mary, who is it, it's not someone from the docks is it Jaysus they only want one ting".

"Yeah, he's from the docks, it's Sean".

"Sean!" she laughed. "Sean, sure he doesn't he never even speaks to me, I say hello to him and he mumbles and scuttles off like a beetle".

"He's just shy, he's been asking about ya, sure you should go and talk to him," replied Mary, smiling, she loved to be a matchmaker.

"What would I talk to him about, besides, me Da would kill me, he's Catholic, you know how he gets".

"Well, he doesn't have to know".

"Yeah and I'd be straight down to the Magdalene laundry, not worth my soul".

"Oh come on one drink with us Saturday, we'll go to a show, be nice, me, you, Jimmy and Sean".

"I don't know. It's awful risky".

"So shall I tell him the good news?".

"I guess so, but what do I tell me Da".

"Tell him you're going out with me, the old drunk, he won't even notice".

"If me Da finds out I'm done for". Milly wrapped her shawl around her tightly as if it was armour. Her father was a tyrant once he had the drink inside him.

They walked to the linen mill, the towers above them loomed. Inside, machines whirled and barefoot children crawled to get the dust and dirt. It was a dangerous job, but their little fingers were the only tools that could clean them.

Mary and Milly walked over to their section and began work. Making sure the reels were moving smoothly and linen was being made for the Titanic. It was beautiful linen, not for the likes of them.

Sheets and pillowcases, tableware, all went through there. The hours were long and the work was hard. Being women, they earned far less and had less job security. The meagre earnings went to the household.

Like the dockyard workers, the women were also affected with hearing loss and lip-reading became the norm. It was hot, noisy and harsh. The women were overseen by the men and had little freedom to improve their status. Life expectancy was low due to the flax getting on the lungs, but what choice did they have.

"Come on, you, start working what are yers on holiday?" bellowed the gaffer Mr Dryden.

"No sir, we just came in. Let me get me shawl off won't ya" bellowed Mary over the machines.

"Oh I do beg ya pardon would ya like a cup of tea as well," he said sarcastically. He wandered off. In Linenopolis, as Belfast was also then known, there was an abundance of mills. Children as young as ten years old worked there between school and at 13 they were full employees. School was a formality as their education did nothing to better themselves. The Millies, the ladies who worked in the mills, strived hard to meet the quotas, there was no time for chatting.

Meanwhile, back at the dock, Jimmy and Michael toiled away. Crouched down all day in a small rat infested area, dirt and grime was their home for the next five years. Their candles lighting up as best they could the plates that they were putting together. Below them, there was a conspiracy afoot regarding Kevin. Mr Bourne was the target. A whistle echoed through, a signal, Jimmy looked. Colin nodded.

Jimmy had to let him know when Bourne was on his way.

"What's that about ?" asked Michael.

"Never you mind," said Jimmy dryly.

"Oh Jimmy, don't be causing no trouble now will ye" implored Michael.

"I'm not, I just gotta tell someone something".

"Tell them what?".

"I just got to let them know when that Bourne is coming, he won't get away with what he did to that lad, besides it's not me, it's someone else," said Jimmy looking out.

"Come on, keep working you've no time to be carrying on".

Jimmy went back to work keeping a careful eye out for the target, as he hammered the rivet his attention was diverted and the hammer came crashing down on his finger!

"Oh ya bastard owww," he shouted, the thumb gushing as it had been squished under Michael's hammer.

"Oh Jaysus and Mary Jimmy, look at that you not watching what ya doing, go quick to the infirmary," yelled Michael.

"Ah screw it, no, I won't they dock me pay, here I'll just band it up I'll deal with it later, carry on, gimme that rag".

He fashioned a bandage out of a dirty old rag and wrapped it crudely around his wound. He couldn't afford to be off work, and though the pain was searing, it was nothing like the pain of hunger you get when you get docked.

"What's going on here then hope you haven't damaged my ship" smiled Bourne as he came to inspect their work.

"Just a flesh wound sir, nothing more," said Jimmy trying to hide the pain in his hand.

"Let me see," said Bourne, carefully examining the wound.

"Really, it's ok I can carry on".

"The hell you can, I don't want your blood on my ship, go to the infirmary, that's five-shilling from you lad," Bourne replied authoritatively.

"But sir," Jimmy implored.

"Don't disobey me, or you want more docked?".

Jimmy sauntered off, that Bourne was going to get it, as he walked down the plank, he saw Andy and Colin.

"He's up there, just seen me bash me finger sent me to the infirmary, didn't want to go and now I'll get docked, make sure you get him good won't ya".

"Oh, you don't gotta worry about that," said Andy throwing his finished cigarette on the ground with venom.

On the way to the infirmary, a nurse was in her office, surprised to see him as men rarely came to see her with injuries that weren't life-threatening.

"Ah, good morning, what do we have here that looks nasty, take a seat," beckoned the nurse. Her bright white uniform, like an angel, sat behind a wooden desk.

"It's nothing missus, but the gaffer seen me and told me to come to you," said Jimmy both apologetically, and with as much masculinity as he could, the pain gave his finger a pulse, and he sucked in the tears.

"That's an interesting bandage you have there, are you hoping for an infection?" smiled the nurse as she unravelled the rag.

"It's nothing really can ya hurry I got work to do".

"You'll not do much work if you don't get it cleaned, wait there," and she turned her back and rummaged for clean bandages and ointment.

"Missus?".

"My name is Nurse Sarah if you please".

"Nurse Sarah, could ya hurry up like".

"Are you so desperate to get away? Here give me your hand".

"Owww," Jimmy whined.

"Don't be a baby, women go through a lot worse with childbirth".

"Oh, it hurts".

"It's going to, you've bruised it something good, this is going to sting a little it's antiseptic," and Nurse Sarah rubbed a cotton bud of the foul-smelling ointment on his dirty bloody hand.

Jimmy jumped in his chair, " Jaysus, that's worse than when I bashed it".

"Some hard dockyard worker you are, there, bandaged up and ready, don't get it wet mind, and keep the bandage on, come and see me the end of the week".

"Thanks missus," and Jimmy ran out the door.

Nurse Sarah smiled to herself. She loved all of her patients, she could only do basic medical care being a woman, but her calming manner did more for the men in her care.

She was a young woman, unmarried and unfazed by the dirt and injuries that were bought her way daily.

The men didn't have a lot of care in their lives and their little visits to her made them smile. To some, it was the only time they could see a doctor or nurse.

Chapter 8

Jimmy's bandaged hand slowed down the work, and the conspiracy

was afoot above. Colin, Andy and No Nose were staking out Mr

Bourne. They watched him prowl from one gang to another,

metering out orders and disappointments.

"Come on, he's coming, pass me that bag," whispered Andy. Colin

passed him the hessian bag and filled it with scraps of heavy metal

leftovers. Tied to the top was a note. 'Bullying bastard' written on it.

Bourne walked ever closer to the landing, where they looked down

on him as he did them. The towering stages above would be easy to

hide the assassins. Everyone had a motive. Everyone stuck together.

Bourne stood directly below them. Perusing the yard, safe that his

power was absolute.

"Drop it now," hissed Colin, No Nose peered out the darkness

watching. The bag plummeted like a stone, straight down in a flash.

"Look out!" someone yelled, and Bourne looked up, the bag coming straight for him, it missed him by millimetres as he fell back, the bag landing with a determined clank. The sweat dripped off Bourne's brow as he realised how close he came to grave injury. His men came running to him,

"Jaysus Mr Bourne are yers alright could have taken you clean out, the lads need to be more careful". They helped him up and he recomposed himself to the angry despot he was. Looking around, all the lads were busying themselves, with a watchful eye on Bourne, not daring to catch his eye. They examined the bag, the note staring at them like angry ghost flapping in the wind.

"Da hell is this shit?" snarled Bourne, he looked around, he knew all eyes were on him, "Get back to work!" he bellowed and walked away. He knew what the note meant. There was nothing he could do, there was no proof, debris always fell. He was not a man to be trifled with. Whether he found the culprit or not, he would have to watch his back from now on.

Chapter 9

The next day Bourne was still fuming about the near-death the day before.

Milly was still anxious about the date with Sean, despite Mary reassuring her that her father wouldn't find out.

Tom Clarke was getting quite a following and tensions were rising. People wanted action.

"The time for the end of English Rule is now. We must fight to the end, who's with me?!".

The crowd roared. Whispers in the wind told of a plot that would start the chain of destruction in Belfast.

"The government pay our men and women nothing, the English keep us in servitude while they dine and rake in the money on the backs of our poverty. We fought and lost under Jim Larkin, and we showed them we have the power! Take back Ireland! Take back Ireland!" chanted the people.

The daily protests on the city hall steps we gaining more followers every day, Belfast would not be silent. The target was chosen. Soon it would be clear to all. A message was being sent.

Hidden in Sailor-town, sat two men. They were miners in a previous town until the mine got shut. They had their own agenda and reasons. Each knew how to make an incendiary device. It was an everyday occurrence in the mines. They had only one goal. To cause havoc and have their voices heard.

"When are we going to do this?" said one.

"Soon," said another.

"Will this be enough to get our message across?" asked the first.

"If not, we'll do it again," they laughed.

The bomb, wires and mesh, gunpowder and nails, it's range would hit many, kill many, injure many and free many.

They sat around it like it was a divine message from God. It sat on the rickety table in the slum, the darkness hiding the evil within.

Sinn Fein, it's claws getting into everyone. Every rebel has a cause. Sailor-town was the centre of operations. It's easy to hide when you are on the edge, an outsider, a stalking panther, ready to strike. The English would be the accelerant.

Guns were being bought in by black-leggers. Ships and trains bringing in ammunitions for a tidy price.

Right under the overlords' noses. Birmingham Irish, the silent partners, across the channel, was thick with Irish patriotism. Peaky Blinders had their price. They got paid a high price. The volcano was bubbling away, waiting.

Another den, guns were being hidden in every nook. Canals and shadows, babies prams, hidden walls, pubs.

The Dockers Rest, the bar where all frequented, was ready to fight. Illegal Gin flowed as plans were drawn.

"Davey, we just had a shipment in, the cellar, 40 guns and bullets, each one for the English," laughed Seamus the landlord, Davey walked through checking the stock, it was quite the armament.

"There's tell of a bomb being made, we gonna be hitting the English, right where it hurts, bastards, there's a new shipment coming tomorrow".

"Tomorrow? Where you think I'm going to store it, have you seen the cellar, this shit needs moving on".

"You're getting paid enough there Seamus, b'sides, it be over soon. Clarke is getting more in and then it be over".

"Be over? It never be over, English rule, I'll be in me grave when it happens, or worse, Crumlin, up the wall with the others".

"Stop ya whining man, I'll see what I can do but the shipment is tonight on the Ballycowan ship, coming through on the Lagan, Jimmy's gonna be helping me, it's come from Birmingham, have you got the gin? We'll pick it up tonight so be ready".

"Yeah 1000 litres right there, Belfast's finest," said Seamus proudly. "Let's have a taste, to Ireland!". They cracked open a case of clear unlabelled bottles and drank the sharp liquid inside, homemade and worth more than any gun, The Peaky Blinders would be making a fortune, a small price to pay in the eyes of the Irish. That night, the ship silently sailed in. Wood, metal, and in the bowels, guns, bullets, gunpowder. The Bulkies examined the ship, they had their price too. For a few pounds, they turned a blind eye. Waved it in. A van was waiting, loaded up, and taken through the back streets. Lights guided the assassins, Jimmy and Davey watched for prying eyes. Seamus opened the cellar and swapped the gin. The cellar was becoming overloaded. But not for long. The return trip, gin was not illegal, but it was suspicious. An eye was watching. Unseen, she hid in the darkness of the alley. Her shawl hiding her face. Briona. She was the eyes of the city and was paid well. A traitor to the cause. Falling back into the night, she had a report to make.

Jimmy walked home. The night air was cool. He saw Andy and his gang with him.

"Andy, evening. Lads," said Jimmy quietly. It was luck that he saw them, they had connections in the city that would prove useful. They walked the streets slowly whilst Jimmy explained his plan, it didn't take long for them to agree to help. Jimmy was getting his secret army together.

Chapter 10

The days wore on. Sean was oblivious to the plot against him.

Jimmy still had yet to tell him about Saturday night and Milly. It

would be fun to tell him. He could hardly contain himself.

"Sean hold up I gotta talk to ya" called Jimmy.

"Morning Jimmy, you look tired. You need to leave that Mary alone

you dorty stop out," Sean said, laughing.

"So, Milly," Jimmy said between breaths as he caught him up.

"Oh God, what now, she never go out wit me, Jimmy, her dad's a

menace".

"See, that's where you're wrong, Mary got her to come out Saturday,

we going to the music hall and she's expecting you".

"Oh no, Jimmy, no, you know I can't," Sean briskly walking, trying

to avoid the subject.

"You're not going to stand her up are ya lad, come on it's just a

laugh, you're coming".

"No way am I. Her dad hates me. He's protestant. I'll burn in hell".

"I can handle him, the old drunk, sides, he never notice".

"Jimmy, no, I'll not go".

"You will go, Saturday, me, you, Mary and Milly, I'm sure you'll mess it up, but it'll be funny come on," said Jimmy patting his back for confidence.

Shaking his head in disbelief, Sean really did like her. With other girls, it didn't matter if he played the fool, but with her, he was a totally different person. He was quiet, charming, aloof. With reluctance, he agreed to go, regretting it already.

"So, why are you so tired what you been up to?".

"Nothing really, just this and that," Jimmy said surreptitiously.

"This and that?" Sean asked, inquisitive.

Sean knew that Jimmy had a hidden side, but they had known each other forever, and it would come out eventually.

"You shouldn't ask questions you don't want the answer to Sean mate, come on or we be late".

Michael was waiting on the corner for them, ready to start the day. It was the end of the week, and today they were to be paid.

It was up to the rivet counter how well for if any rivets were even slightly out, or materials were damaged even if not through their own fault, they would be debited for the replacements. It was always a source of indignation, and tempers flared.

"That bastard better not screw us today. We worked like a slave all week".

"Son, it be fine, Sean'll be needing the money for his date with Milly," he said laughing, Jimmy was smiling, and Sean looked away nervously pretending not to hear.

The idle wind ran through the yard amongst the sooty faces that toiled in the darkness. Men aged beyond their early years, boys who wouldn't live to be what we would call old, blackened lungs and toughened skin.

Below them, Bourne was walking around, still seething that he nearly got injured. He needed to find the culprit to restore his position on the site. He couldn't be seen as weak and his minions would help.

"I'll hang that bastard if it's the last thing I do," he scowled to one.

"We've not heard anything," said Quint.

"Well, keep an eye out, I reckon it's those lot, the Riordan's, lazy Catholics, can't trust none of them".

Looking up to the skies, the men toiled, Jimmy looked below at Bourne, eyeing him with suspicion. Jimmy wasn't scared of him and knew he would be part of his downfall one day.

"Jimmy come on, get on with it, if he sees ya, ya be for it," shouted Sean over the hammering.

"He's planning something".

"Whatever it is, you'll see soon enough come on".

Sam rushed in with more rivets. Running through the tunnels of the ship from the forge with hot rivets in hand, his time was limited. It was a treacherous run through debris and metal. Trips and falls were not uncommon, and neither was death, for 17 men and boys had already been killed building the Ship Of Dreams before she even launched.

Sam ran down to James, for more rivets, and they treated it like a game to see who could get more done. It was dangerous, but this camaraderie was common, and in a time where fun was alcohol-fuelled, this was a cheaper alternative.

"Come on James, we be sure to do more today, the rivet counter coming later!" shouted Michael.

"I'm going as fast as I can, here!" and handed the rivet to him. Sam took it and ran as fast as his rickety legs could carry him. Through the darkness, the orange glow lighting his way. Dodging beams and sparks, leaping over gangways he made to his team, one wrong step, and he would be done for but, he had made this journey hundreds of times a day and knew it well enough to avoid danger.

"Sam, you be careful lad running like that," Michael yelled. It was too loud to be kind in whispers.

"I be ok, granddad," the cheeky young lad replied.

"Don't granddad me ya little gob shite just be careful ya hear".

Sam ran back as they hammered in the rivet, one after the other, black sweat pouring from tired faces. If not for the whites of the eyes, they would be invisible to all.

The day wore on, and the horn went for lunch, and as usual, pieces came out, filled with all sorts of left over's. Each inspecting each other for swaps and gossip.

They all sat in their groups, catching up with each other like geese, listening to hear and not hear; it was not all good gossip. Trouble was brewing in the city, and hushed tones had plans.

"So what we having today then lads" bounded a wall of a man. This was Arthur. A giant man who would eat you if you stood still enough. He swiped a man's sandwich and ate it in one bite. The man sat there, starved but amazed.

Sean and Jimmy watched astounded. "Who the hell is that?".

"That's Arthur, one of the ironworkers, greedy bastard, they say he could eat a whole cow, bell and all, he must have hollow legs".

"And does he always steal ya lunch?" asked Jimmy.

"You want to stand up to him," said Sean.

"Ya'd need a crane to stand up to that, look at the size of him, I feel like a leprechaun," laughed the hungry man.

In the distance, you could hear a man complaining about his lunch, and his mates laughing.

"If I eat a cabbage sandwich again, I swear I'll jump off the nearest gantry".

"Tell ya Mrs to make sometin else den" laughed his friends.

"It's not her who makes it though" to a crowd of laughter".

"Who makes it then?" said another.

"I do, and I hates cabbage," throwing his sandwiches back his box.

The men all laughed; though they had little choice in their life, there were still fun times and closeness, and they all shared what little they had.

The giant moved on man to man to steal what food they had, except the one with the cabbage, even he wouldn't touch that.

Whispers and plans to halt the giant's wave of gluttony were echoing through the crowds, they all worked hard, he was one man. They couldn't match his strength but, like David and Goliath, they had more whit.

Chapter 11

Belfast police had eyes everywhere but being paid by the English. They were less popular and their job more difficult to find anything out about what was happening in the city, Sailor-town, notoriously the hive of all action was closed to outsiders, except one.

Briona had seen Jimmy and his lot. She had no scruples of dobbing people in, money was tight, and everyone had their price.

She walked into the station to see Chief Inspector Lovett. It's easy to be ignored in this part of town, and no one of her kind would go there willingly.

Victorian woodwork greeted her. It was different for her to be there on the other side of the cells. Officer O'Hanlon walked her into the office, Lovett was looking out the window. His silhouette was formidable. Pipe smoke surrounding him. A tall, mustached, typical Irish man, he held little respect for the people he was supposed to protect, his bosses needed results. He eyed her with suspicion as he sat in his chair.

"Briona, what do you have for me?" he asked, emptying his pipe and refilling it.

Her anger inside echoed through her eyes. Her kind was worthless. Not just because she was a female, but she was working-class uneducated Irish and Catholic, what she lacked she made up for in whit. It is easy to be unseen when you are nothing.

"I have information for you, but it's going to cost ya," she said and sat in the wooden chair as if she was his equal.

"Very well," he said. Opening his desk drawer, he pulled out a bag of coins and threw them on the table. She picked them up, and they chinked in her hand. Their weight felt like they were more than she would earn making lace for the rich in Linenopolis.

A pause. "Well, spit it out, girl I don't have time for this".

"Fine, I saw the guns, and I saw who took em, too," she said.

His eyes lit up. Finally, a decent lead. He had no choice but to believe her.

"And?".

"Jimmy, Jimmy Mahon, I didn't see the other fella, but they came from the dock".

"Where did they go?" writing in his little pad everything she was saying.

"I didn't see it. I just saw it drive off".

"Were you seen?".

"You think I'd still be breathing if I was?".

Briona knew her position was precarious, and she wasn't wrong, if she were found to be an informer, death would be a relief from the suffering she would endure.

Lovett got up from his desk and looked out the window. Surveying his land and it's peoples, he knew a plan was afoot, and Briona was a great help. He felt pity for her; he wouldn't show it.

He walked around to her and sat on the edge of the desk like a kind teacher.

"Briona, I need you to find out where they went, you wouldn't lie to me, would you?" he stared into her eyes, trying to work her out.

"Lie to ya? Now, why would I do that, listen if you don't believe me that's your lookout, I told ya what I saw," she said indignantly.

He grabbed her arm and pulled her up, holding her against the wall. This was not the first time Briona had been hurt at the hands of a man, being a woman it was common. She was strong enough now to take anything he could give her.

His tobacco breath was flowing in her face, his wide eyes and yellow teeth centimetres from her.

"It's the truth, get off me!" she struggled to shake him off, he held her tight. He could do what he wanted. His eyes met hers, he had some kindness in him, but he needed to be sure she was being truthful, he let her go.

"Find out where those guns are, why they need them, I'll pay you double if you get anything good, get out, I'm busy," and he sat down in his wooden chair, and turned again to his window. She stood there redundant, yearning for respect, for him to see her as a person, not a street urchin. She picked up her money and left. But, like she had seen Jimmy, she was also seen and spied upon. Eyes were everywhere.

O ' Hanlon walked in and closed the door.

"Sir?" he asked.

"O'Hanlon, Jimmy Mahon, you know him?".

"Only vaguely sir, he works at the docks on the ship, why?".

"See if you can't find out anything about some guns coming into the city, don't be too obvious about it, something's going down, we need to find out what before it happens, we don't want a repeat of last year".

"No sir, I'll see what I can do".

O'Hanlon was a good officer and wanted to go far, as an Irish Constabulary man, he too had to be careful, people saw his uniform, not him.

Chapter 12

Back at the dock, the day was coming to an end, and the rivet
counter was doing his rounds, eyes watched him.

"Come on lads, lets get these in, might be able to top it up, more
money for Sean and his sweetheart tonight," laughed Michael.

"Would you shut it, man I'm nervous enough," piped Sean.

The rivet counter, Mr Collins, came round with his board, inspecting
to the sounds of shouting and protests, he decided if the work was
good enough and how much you got paid, your pay was a pittance
anyway, and his influence would make it much more or much less.
He approached the Riordan team.

"Let's have a look then lads, out the way," and he peered at their
work, his candle lighting the steel rivets.

"There's nothing wrong Mr Collins, you'll see all done correctly,"
claimed Michael humbly.

"I'll be the judge of that thank you, here look, that rivet, not pushed
in enough and the outside of it damaged where you've tried to
hammer it in, but it cooled too quick, that'll cost ya, it'll need to be
removed, and re-put in," and he marked it on his board.

"Come on, that's not fair that rivets fine," protested Sean.

"Is that right is it, I'll just go tell the managers that it's ok to have shoddy OK work on the world's finest ship, then shall I, better still you want to tell them, please feel free". Collins stood there glaring at them, his patronising manner flowed through him, he felt like he was above them in all things.

Michael, who never stood up to anyone, even surprised himself for speaking up. Working with tough men made him forget he was a tired old man. He shook his head. There's was nothing he could do and was lucky to have a job. Mr Collins moved on.

Like a wave of ill-feeling, the hard toil became harder when the men were found to be at fault. It was the hardest job to do and the least paid. The lads began to remove the rivet and worked hard to replace it. It was harder to remove than it was to fit, but thankfully it was only one.

Their day had ended, and it seemed it would not get any better. As they walked to the office to the pay, the crowds began to gather. They were being prevented from leaving by Bourne. He wanted answers, and knowing the lads and the draw of the pub, the answer would come quick.

Harland and Wolff were watching from their office. They didn't deal much with the workforce. They had no need to. They watched with curious eyes; a fight would soon break out. They asked their office junior to take a look and report back, but be careful, he was a pencil pusher and had no toughness about him.

Clean porcelain skin, Anderson glowed amongst the blackened faces, he approached them with caution and respect. They were a gang not to be messed with.

"Hey, what's going on what's all this?" he asked.

"They won't let us through to get out wages and go home, Bourne is stopping everyone, he wants to know who dropped something on him I don't know".

"Bourne? Who that man there, fuck sake! Let me through," and he waded through the crowds to get to him. "You got to let these men go, Harland sent me," shouted Anderson in his crisp white shirt.

"Oh, go back to your desk this doesn't concern you!" yelled Bourne.

"The hell it doesn't, open these gates, or I'll get the Bulkies," Anderson yelled back. His small, clean stature was standing firm.

"Get them, someone here nearly killed me last week, and I want to know who" shouted Bourne.

The crowd was getting more agitated and tighter as more bodies gathered on the already weakening bridge. It was only there for traffic, not for standoffs.

"Open the fuckin gates dammit, move it!" yelled men in the crowd.

"Who dropped that bag! I just need one name!" ordered Bourne. Anderson retreated, he knew he would be of no use and reported back to Harland.

"Who is this Bourne? Anderson, call the constabulary to get them down here and sort this out, we can't have this, we have a reputation to protect, can't have a gang of Navvies holding us up, move it man!". Harland was disturbed. He liked order and efficiency, he respected his men and hoped that it was mutual.

The bridge beneath the men cracked and creaked, the water below like a starving crocodile waiting for its meal, shouts, and push's, Bourne laughing at the power he had. Crash! Bodies fell to the sea below, men hung on to the sides, splashing in the darkness, looks of horror on faces in the black water, screams for help, hands pushing through searching for land!

Man upon man, trying to get out, some trying to get in to rescue those who could not swim, the bridge, it's splinters in the water too small to act as a life raft. Hands grabbing men, pulling them to safety. Michael and Sean were leaning over, pulling up men. Lungs filled with water, white faces, bloated, and staring at the sky above, they lulled on top of the water, their numbers increasing. Bourne stood and watched, incredulous as to what happened. Sirens in the air, the constabulary, ambulances, helping those who needed it, piles of bodies lined the docklands, blankets laid out, coughing, newly white faces bathed with seawater trembled in the cold, wives running to the crowds to help, Harland and Wolff watching in despair, how could this happen? Bourne and his men disappeared into the shadows, this was their fault, and they would be for it.

The screams became silent as the last of the 40 bodies were dragged out, coughs and splutters, tears flowed, this was another tragic, tragic episode in the making of the Ship Of Dreams.

Chapter 13

Michael, Jimmy, and Sean sloshed home, silent, shocked. Opening the door slowly, they walked in.

"Mary mother and Joseph, what happened to yous?" exclaimed Ma. Michael dropped into his chair, Mary kneeling beside him, eyeing the other two.

"What happened? Why you all wet? What're all the sirens? I'll put the kettle on", the solution to all life's ills.

"The bridge collapsed, Bourne wouldn't let us pass, men fell in the dock, so many didn't make it, there'll be trouble for this, Jaysus Mary it was terrible, I never heard such screams in all me life" cried Michael.

"Mary, it was the worst thing I ever saw," said Jimmy, and nothing ever bothered him. He supped his tea, and Sean was silent. He sat at the table, just staring off into space.

"Sean, lad you, ok? Here have this tea, it's ok," said Ma, she treated him like her own, she was a lovely woman who would care for anyone and everyone. She'd give you her last penny.

She put a gentle arm around him, and he closed his eyes momentarily. He'd never seen anything like this before.

At the dock, bodies were being moved to the morgue. Tears were flowing, Lovett over-saw, he was always on duty, and, hopefully, none of the dead were of use to him in finding the guns.

"O'Hanlon, make a list of the dead, send it to the papers, let them deal with it, have you found anything about these guns?".

"Not yet sir".

"No doubt this might be a trigger so keep your ear to the ground, send some men over to Harland, explain what happened. Jesus, what a day".

He sat and sighed. He was right.

The next day it made the front page. Photos of the dead laid out for all to see. Work must still carry on. The ship still needed to be built. Its gates would still open.

Harland and Wolff sat; they needed to be very careful. If they failed, they would be at risk. The ship would be at risk.

"Good lord man, this is all we need," said Ismay reading the morning papers. His men were sitting ahead of him, Harland and Wolff. The shipbuilders had to act quickly and carefully. They had lost many men, and to do nothing may delay the ship and ruin them. "We need to act if we are want to stay on schedule. I can't believe this has happened, those men, can't they just work and stop with these games. Who is this Bourne fellow? I keep hearing his name and not in terms that polite society would welcome".

Harland answered. He had his ear to the ground and was on the workers' side. If they were happy, he was happy, and the ship would be built on time.

"He's one of the foremen, keep the lads in line, but sometimes the power goes to his head as I hear it".

"He needs bringing down. I won't have one man ruin all we have worked for because of a power trip. Harland, send one of the lads to go and bring him in I'll have a word with him. Wolff, any ideas what we can do?".

"I think we should take a day of rest for the lost and compensate the families, as a goodwill gesture".

"Compensation? Hmm, that sounds like the way to go. We can't afford a day of rest. We must stick to the plan". Ismail sighed with disbelief as he re-read the paper. He could not believe that something like this could happen, what was happening to his beloved shipyard. They drew plans for compensation to the grieving families and would hold a memorial for them. To some, this was heartfelt. To others, it was not enough. It was never enough.

It was a quiet day despite the previous night's events. Taking their pay seemed cruel; their hard work felt like they had been punished rather than rewarded. But they couldn't say no, they needed money. The pub was packed. Jimmy, Sean, and Michael sat in the corner quietly. Jimmy was playing out in his head the plan. He eyed Seamus at the bar, O'Hanlon was also drinking at the bar incognito, ever listening. This was the centre for the men who worked at the dock, so it would stand to sense he would hear something of use. It's easy to be missed when you want to be.

Jimmy headed to the bar and snuck in the back with Seamus. Seamus shut the door behind him.

"Jimmy, I heard something today, someone was seen talking to that Chief Inspector. It's getting dangerous, I think he knows, I think we're being watched," said Seamus worriedly.

"Who was it?" asked Jimmy.

"Davey, he was in the drunk tank, he saw some woman, he said she works at the mill, we need to get these out of here Jimmy it's getting too much".

"Ok, leave it with me. I'll see what I can do, keep this quiet though, do you know who she was?".

"He didn't get her name, but she was your Mary's age. They must know each other".

"It's not like I can ask her, I'll keep an eye, I'll be in touch".

Jimmy left and went to his seat. O'Hanlon watched him out the corner of his eye. His ears pricked up. He watched Seamus, he drank up and left. It was all coming together. The lads also drank up and left, going their separate ways.

Jimmy walked the quiet streets to Sailor-town. No Nose smoked under an orange light, and Jimmy entered a squalid little house. The lads were waiting on Jimmy's word.

"We got a problem, Davey was in the drunk tank and saw a woman with Lovett, she seen us".

"Who is she?" asked Colin.

"I don't know, but she works at the mill, Seamus needs the stuff moving, we need to find her to shut her up".

"There's another shipment coming in soon, where we gonna put that?" asked Andy through a haze of smoke. He had panic in his voice.

"We'll put them by the old canal, it's dark at the end of the Queens, no one ever goes there as its too far from anything, they'd never find it there, we'll leave it there until it's go time, it won't be long".

"The bombs nearly been made," said one.

Jimmy nodded. The plan was coming to fruition and time was getting short, people were arming themselves, as long as his family were safe and not in the know they would be ok.

He left and walked home.

Chapter 14

The Sunday walk to church was a solemn one full of tears. Bodies still laying in morgues still to be collected. Father Patterson stood in his pulpit, looking over his flock in their Sunday best. Sad looking faces, it would be a hard time for the women, the breadwinners of some were now gone, and their future looked bleak.

Ismail sat in the office. He had to carry on building the ship, and deaths would not get in his way, he had to answer to people too. "Take a letter," he said to his secretary. Pencil in hand, she wrote his words. He sighed whilst looking out the window at the ship as it was being built.

"To the families of those lost in this disaster, please accept my most deepest condolences and know that you will be compensated. Your men will not be forgotten for their sacrifice, and we will learn very valuable lessons from this. Signed".

The words, though he meant them, seemed hollow, times were hard for the working class as it was, and in this city of two religions, it was even harder, being English, he too had to be careful. He carried on looking at his ship, his legacy, how many more would die?

His letter was published in the papers across Belfast. To some, it was a kind gesture, to others, an insult.

"Very valuable lessons, bloody English!" shouted one. Tom Clarke read with curious eyes, he could use this to his advantage on the steps at Speakers Corner to gain support to rid Ireland of the English once and for all.

"Is this what our men are worth?!" he bellowed, waving the paper above his head like a red rag to a bull. The crowd jeered.

"Pay off our families while their men lie on cold metal slabs, they just carry on! No more will we stand for this treatment, we will drive out the English, we will get retribution for their deaths, they will be martyrs for that Ship Of English Dreams, they will be avenged, many may suffer so that one day all Irish people may know justice and peace!".

The Constabulary was watching, as was Lovett. Clarke would be valuable to find out where the guns were hidden. Briona was not part of the inner circle. Lovett would have to get Clarke and Jimmy, but there were laws to be obeyed, and you couldn't just arrest anyone without cause. He had to be smart.

Father Patterson read humble words from his bible, imploring people not to seek revenge, lowly weeps echoed, hymns were sung, and they all shuffled off home.

The brotherhood was meeting. Their time to strike was soon, and they had their target.

Seamus grew worried. He knew he was being watched and needed to be as far away from the guns as possible. Jimmy had moved them in the night, Briona had not seen where.

She walked the quiet streets, she had no one to miss, and no one would miss her either.

Informers were replaceable. Lovett looked over the city, one tragedy replaced another, but it was the big one he was trying to prevent. He couldn't fail. He didn't have a choice in that.

The bells rang across the city as a mark of respect for the dead. Cemeteries had new residents. Ship 401 was coming together. Two sides were vowing revenge.

Chapter 15

Monday was a solemn one. The work still needed to be done. James lit the furnaces, and Sam waited for the team. He stood smoking his morning cigarette, a kid of 15, he was a man. There was no time for games. Even his meagre earnings helped his mam a little.

Bourne walked about, as usual, his minions by his side, they were a target now. It was their fault the bridge collapsed, sinister eyes observed them.

No Nose watched through the smoke, always listening, always watching. When people think you're stupid, they will have loose lips and underestimate your power.

Something was brewing, an itch to be scratched. Whispers of Catholic plots and Protestant revenge.

Jimmy was called over, Colin, Andy, and No Nose were casually having a cigarette before work.

"Lads," said Jimmy.

"Bourne," said Colin.

"What about him?".

"He needs taking out, you in?".

"Sure".

"Tonight, when the shift clocks out, we get him then, Prod bastard! I doubt we have any trouble",

"What about his mates?".

"They leave early today I heard, we get him then".

The group wandered their separate ways.

One of the office juniors walked to Bourne and quietly asked for his attendance in the office. The lads watched, trying to read the lips to see what was being said. Bourne's muffled anger echoed through the waves, and he walked on with the junior.

Bourne made his way up the wooden stairs wiping his brow, nervous like a schoolboy on his way to the headmasters' office.

He knocked on the door and was called in. Ismail sat at his desk, glaring at Bourne.

"Bourne?" asked Ismail.

"Yes sir," replied Bourne, standing to attention, cap in hand.

"Take a seat. Bourne, I have heard a lot about you around the yard, none of it good. Tell me, what happened with this bridge collapse".

"Well sir, the lads, they nearly dropped a weight on me head, would have killed me if my team hadn't have said, I wanted to find out who it was so I stopped them getting the pay until the culprit stepped forward. How was I to know that the bridge would collapse".

"Someone tried to kill you?" asked Ismail, disbelieving what he is hearing.

"Yes sir, they filled a bag with bolts and dropped it".

"How do you know it wasn't an accident?".

"I just know sir. Them lads the Catholics you can't trust them at all sir I had to show them I am boss".

"You are the boss? You? Pray if you are boss, then what does that make me?" anger rising in his voice.

"Sir I only meant". Ismail cut him off.

"You listen to me Bourne. I run this dock, and you work for me, and if you have any grievances, you raise them through the proper channels! Do you realise what you have done? Not only has your idiocy lost me a great deal of workforce, but you have risked the reputation of this yard, myself and Belfast!". His anger at full rage that made Bourne sink back into his chair.

"Sir". Looking at his lap like a naughty schoolboy.

"I haven't finished. Because of you, I now have to compensate the families who you have left fatherless and sonless because of your childish and megalomaniac ways, and where will that money come from? I'll tell you where. You. You will be docked two weeks' salary, and you will work double shifts until further notice, and if I so much as hear your name in this office ever again, God help me I will use you as the anchor of this ship do you hear me!". Ismail's face was crimson with rage. Bourne was silent and close to tears. He was not used to being told off. He was powerless in this room.

"I'm very sorry sir. It's them Catholics sir, you have to watch them," Bourne said imploringly twisting his cap in his hands.

"Get out," said Ismail bluntly. Bourne stood up quietly, thanked him, and left. He was quiet for the rest of the day.

At the mill, Mary and Milly were chatting about Sean and the accident.

"I don't know what's going to happen, thank God Sean and Jimmy were there, Da might not have made it".

"It doesn't bear thinking about, listen about our night out. I don't think I'm going to go now," said Milly.

"Oh why not? It's just what ya need a night out, ya never come out".

"Ya know".

"Your dad, oh he won't know".

"He will, and I be out of here straight to Donegal Magdalene laundry, you know how he feels about Catholics".

"Well, just don't tell him".

"And what if we get married?".

"Milly, it's one date. It's not ya wedding".

"I know, but you don't know where it can lead".

"Come out Milly. We'll look after ya". Mary was looking at her with begging eyes. After a while, Milly agreed to go. Her dad couldn't control everything she did; she was a grown woman, after all.

"No, I'll go, I just got to watch for me da, he go spare". This was the first time Milly had defied her dad, and though terrified of him finding out, she was excited to go out.

They carried on through the noise of the machines, how they heard each other at all, and when the dusty machines went off the ringing carried on in their heads.

Briona watched them. She was not as discreet as she hoped. Mary caught her eye.

"Sure what she looking at?" she nodded to Milly.

"That Briona, don't trust her, I heard she's in with the RIC".

"If she keeps eyeing me up, I'll mess widj her".

At the dock, a plan was forming. The bell went for dinner and big Arthur on the hunt for food again. Over he went to the weakest man who had the best looking sandwiches. Jimmy and his mates watched. The man was one of theirs, and his sandwiches though thick with soft white bread and the best bacon, also had part of the ship laced inside.

As Arthur bit into the sandwich, his teeth engaged with the metal and broken teeth. He spat out the contents as they clanged on the floor to the riotous laughter of the men, like children in a playground who had foiled the bully, Arthur dashed off to the infirmary. He never stole food again.

That afternoon, the lads watched as Bourne left and they stalked behind him. Still shaken but frustrated at his reprimand, Bourne didn't hear them come behind him. Andy put his arm around him and dragged him into an alley while Colin and Jimmy followed closely. No Nose the loyal watchdog.

"What you doing get off me!" yelled Bourne.

"Ya fucking murderer!" yelled Andy as the lads kicked him. Colin raining blows on his now bloody face with his boot.

Bourne tried to defend himself but his legs wouldn't get him up.

Lying in a pool of blood, Andy, Colin and Jimmy watched him writhe.

"Fucking prole," and Jimmy spat at him.

"You pull any more shit, and I fucking kill ya, ya hear me!" shouted Jimmy. Gurgling in his blood, the lads walked off as if nothing had happened. Bourne would not bother them again.

Chapter 16

In Sailor-town, the bomb sat and waited for its instructions. The ship was being built within walking distance.

Milly and Mary walked home and they felt that they were being followed, looking behind Briona was following. Mary turned and yelled, "You got a problem there, Briona?".

"No, do you?" she said, aggressively walking over.

"Come on Mary, let's go," pulled Milly.

"No, I want to know what her problem is".

"How's your Jimmy?" asked Briona.

"Jimmy? Why? What's he got to do with you?".

"I heard he has some dealings I'd watch if I were you".

"What you mean, 'dealings'? I'd watch yerself if I were you Fenian whore".

"Watch who you call whore Mary least I'm not a traitor".

"Traitor? Who's the traitor".

"You go ask Jimmy I'm sure he knows more".

Briona smiled and walked off. All she needed was to plant the seed and watch it grow. She wanted to know where those guns were just as much as Lovett. It could change her world.

Mary walked home and made tea. Jimmy walked in loud and boastful as usual, Mary needed to speak to him in private but in a small house, it was nigh on impossible.

"Oh Mary, are you a sight for sore eyes, are you making a cuppa?".

"I am, I'm not running a café though, come and help me".

Jimmy leaned on the side next to her to wash some cups. He could feel there was something unsaid.

"You ok Mary, something bothering you?".

"I spoke to Briona today, she said something about you".

"About me? What did she says sure I've never even spoken to her".

"Never spoke to her?".

"No, never, what's this about?".

"She said you were a traitor".

Jimmy's demeanour changed. His eyes blackened. She needed taking out, she was a loose cannon and he couldn't have Mary involved.

"Traitor? Traitor to who, sure she be winding you up Mary, I don't even know her".

"Jimmy, I know you, you wouldn't lie to me, would ya?". Mary's eyes were looking into his, trying to work him out.

"Sure would I lie to you. I love you, Mary come on, get that tea on I'm parched and less of this nonsense".

"Jimmy, I mean it". Mary grabbed his wrist at the sink.

"I'm no traitor Mary, I don't know who she is and there are things I can't tell you, you have to trust me," his tone has grown dark and serious.

"Jimmy, I.".."

"Mary, don't ask me anything, ok, I can't tell you".

Mary sighed, deep down she knew he was planning something and now Briona knew about it, there was nothing she could do except hope for the best.

Jimmy sat drinking his tea. Briona had to go. The fire crackled and the clock ticked. It was like a timer, his bomb was already primed. It wouldn't be long now.

Jimmy walked home to Sailor-town. The UVF members sat around smoking, talking of the bomb.

Theft was not uncommon in Belfast. Ship paint, taps, linens, once there were an amnesty and all stolen goods were to be returned without question or punishment, well, what they didn't expect was that the Irish were honest folk and bought too much back so that there was nowhere to store the newly returned goods and so the amnesty was revoked and people could just keep their stolen property.

"Bloody ell Andy when does ya house launch?" laughed Jimmy, the walls red and black, and nice linens on the furniture.

Over beer they laughed, comrades.

"We got problems. I know who the snitch is".

"Who is it like?" asked Colin.

"Names Briona works at the mill with Mary, been letting my Mary know all sorts of things, talking to that Lovett, feck sake".

"Shall we postpone the hit?".

"Feck no, it'll all go as planned. She needs taking out".

"It's not Briona Duffy by any chance is it?" asked Andy.

"Yeah, why you know her?".

"Ha yeah, I know her, father died last year in the riots, mother ended up in the madhouse, just her now".

"You need to take her out, here," and Jimmy passed his gun to him.
The plan was hatched to get her after work. The UVF were warriors, and they acted quickly.

"We have a final shipment coming from Birmingham as well, another 40 guns and ammo. The warehouse on Queens, we store them there then when it's time, we strike".

They drank a toast to a free Ireland, brothers in arms.

"We are now on the threshold of a newer movement, with a newer hope and inspiration lads,

to Ireland," and they clinked the whiskey and their plans came together.

Briona Duffy would sell her observations no more.

Chapter 17

Briona walked home through the gas-lit streets. Buildings, tall and empty. When the factories were closed up, it was a ghost town. She was confident in herself. She was intelligent and tough. She knew she was being followed.

Footsteps on cobbles behind her. Her steps quickened as did theirs. "Briona Duffy!?" shouted the voice. It was familiar to her. It was Andy. She was too close to Jimmy for it to be safe; if he missed, she could identify Jimmy.

Footsteps became running, darting into an alley and hiding in the darkness, her heart beating like a terrified fox on a moor. The assailant's voice was echoing through. He passed her without notice. Slowly she stood up behind him, stealthy, reached in her shawl and grabbed her knife and, without hesitation, drove it into his back.

The sharpness, at first unrecognisable, blood oozing out of the wound, Andy turned around to see her staring at him, he went down, grabbed her shawl, she fell on top, stabbing him again with ferocity, his gun redundant at his side, he could not believe that such a weak woman could end him this way. Her face smiling at him was the last thing he saw. He was a message to the brotherhood, don't mess with Briona Duffy. She was now in even more danger.

Chapter 18

Back at the docks, the ship was coming on, the sides were now built and getting higher, and the idle wind stronger the higher the men climbed.

"Ah tis the closest we get to heaven aye lads," shouted Sean.

"Yeah you better watch out there. It's a fair drop. Sam, you watch out now no messing" Michael was protective of the young lad, he'd seen many slip over and fall to their deaths. The working class was just replaceable numbers to them.

Metal sheets were pulled in to line. Rivets were hammered in, each with sweat and hard work and worry, and it would all be for not. Cranes overhead carrying the ship like a dress pattern ready to be put together.

Below, the boilermakers were fitting the heart of the ship. 29 boilers to move a ship of this size,

rudder's bigger than a house with blades that looked fearsome when being fitted, metal on metal, fires burned and the ship was being given birth to and finally taking shape.

Flat-capped men and boys without safety harnesses worked above, steadying themselves not to slip. Your workmate today could be in a grave tomorrow. Sammy ran to the team to deliver yet another rivet, most famous ship in the world next to the Arc some would say.

"Sammy, would you be careful feck's sake" yelled Michael again.

"Whatever granddad I be fine watch" as Sam balanced on the edge, clowning around, vaulting and laughing. Didn't bother him that 200 feet below was certain death. Though he was a man by then he was also still a child.

He jumped down and ran for the next rivet.

"That boy be the death of me," said Michael wiping his brow.

"Sean, when's ya date with young Milly?".

Sean had hoped this had been forgotten about, sadly with Jimmy on his side, this was not to be.

"That's Saturday, Mr Riordan".

"Oh young love, hey Jimmy".

"Yeah Michael".

"So, where you taking her?".

"We going to a show at the Palace".

"That be nice. I used to take Mary's mother there when we were courting".

"Is that right Mr Riordan?".

"Many a true romance started there me lad".

"Mmm maybe".

Sean was still nervous. She wasn't like the other girls he'd been with, this one he cared about.

At the mill, Mary was chatting to Milly about Briona.

"She not in today?".

"No one seen her, she probably just late".

"I asked Jimmy about her. He's never heard of her little tramp trying to come between us. When she comes in, I'll tell her so".

"Sure you will not she's not worth it Mary, she might not even work here anymore if she carries on being late".

"Is she often late?".

"Oh yeah she's always late no one knows where she is it's not like she has a family to look after, I feel sorry for the poor girl".

"Why you feel sorry for her, she's a trouble maker".

"Well, that business with her ma and her dad dying the way he did".

"Well, he should have been more careful. It was a dangerous time, everyone shooting each other and for what, nothing changed".

"No, nothing really changed, but they saw that we had a voice".

"Guess so".

"Get back to work!!" yelled the foreman, walking about, angry eyes met his and he scuttled off, he had power but with women, he was scared of them. Hell hath no fury like a woman scorned was a phrase he knew too well.

They watched the machines produce the linen, rolls and rolls of white lace pillowcases, sheets, and crisp table cloths for the ship.

"Milly, are yers excited about Saturday?".

"Saturday?".

"Oh don't tell me ya forgot, your date with Sean".

"Oh that, yeah I don't think I'll go".

"Och come one why not?".

"I'm still scared me da find out. It's not worth it".

"Come on, he never find out and Sean's dead excited to see ye".

"Shut up. He is not".

"He is, won't stop talking about it to Jimmy".

"Oh no, Mary it's gonna be horrible".

"It's one night Milly, come on".

Milly was going, but reluctantly, one date she thought, and that would be the end of it.

"Yes, I'm still going, but no promises".

Chapter 19

'Ok da I'm just off out" yelled Milly by the door, hoping her dad
would be too drunk to get to her.

"Milly! Get in here where you off to?".

"I told you dad, I'm going to the Palace with Mary".

"That Catholic whore you are not!".

"She's not a whore dad!" Yelled Milly, backing away. He was his
usual drunk self, staggering up to belt her. It was not a rare
occurrence to feel his wrath at the end of a piece of leather.

"Don't you answer me back girl get up them stairs!".

"I will not. I'm going out. I be back later!". Her heart beating
rapidly, she was scared, and tears began to form, but she had to stand
up for herself.

"You go out that door you won't be coming back". he yelled as she
slammed the door. Tears were running down her pretty pale face.
His threats were empty. She was all he had since she was a wee girl
and times were hard for both of them. Her feelings contradicted
themselves. She hated how he was, but he was all she had, so she
had to keep him with her.

Milly scurried to the town, trying to look presentable, all she needed now was to look like she had been crying on a first date. The normal thing to do was cry after it.

Sean, on the other hand, had no such trouble. Except what he put himself through. Standing in front of the mirror, examining every nook and cranny of his face that one would never think to see before suddenly became glaringly obvious to him. Pulling his tie this way and that, practicing his smile and having imaginary conversations with Milly, Jimmy burst in making him jump.

"Jesus Mary and Joseph, you scared the hell outta me!".

Laughing, Jimmy grabbed Sean and ruffled his hair.

"Come on, or we be late".

"Jimmy, how do I look?".

"You look beautiful like a summers rose come on," said Jimmy laughing.

"Jimmy, I'm serious you think this is ok?".

Jimmy examined him, pulled his face and said: "You'll do".

"Cheers mate, that's just what I need, feck sake".

"I don't know why you're so nervous you been out with loads of girls".

"Yeah, but none of them was Milly McCaffery".

"Come on lad". Out the door, they flew.

Chapter 20

Excitement was in the air. Lights and laughter of the bars and pubs. Couples walking down the street, the Palace was beckoning for the evening's entertainment. Milly and Mary were waiting outside.

"Hey Milly don't you look lovely. Have you been crying? Has your dad had a go again, that bastard!".

"It's fine, God, do I look terrible?".

"No, you look great, really pretty," said Mary.

"I really should go home dad was in a fearsome temper when I told him I was meeting you".

"You didn't mention Sean did ya?".

"No, I just said you".

"Did he call me a Catholic whore again?" said Mary smiling. It didn't bother her at all what he called her. He was a drunk and his opinion worthless.

"I'm sorry".

"Don't be, he's right", and they both laughed. The night air was sweet with ale and ginger snaps from the street sellers. Sean and Jimmy dodged through the crowd and met the girls.

"Ladies," said Jimmy smiling, putting an arm around Mary and kissing her cheek.

"Hi there, hey Sean you look very dapper tonight, doesn't he Milly?", Milly, just looking like a shy child.

"Hi Sean, Jimmy".

"Hey Milly" mumbled Sean, Jimmy shook his head smiling.

"Shall we go in get a drink and a seat before the show starts?".

"Yeah great idea, I need a drink," said Mary and took Jimmy's arm. Milly took Sean's arm but her delicate nature, Sean daren't hold it too tight for fear it might break into a thousand pieces.

The chandeliers dazzled, cigar smoke rose from the bar, a buzz of indistinct voices echoed through the foyer. Music played from pianos as they warmed up for the night's entertainment the great stage singer Nelly Pope.

"So Milly, have you been here before?" asked Sean trying to make small talk.

"No never, have you?".

"Once or twice, it's a good show they put on you'll love it".

"I hope so". Milly was trying to relax. At the back of her mind, she could hear her father berating her.

"How's your dad? I hope you didn't have any trouble coming out?".

"No more than usual, I can handle him". What choice did she have, she thought.

"If he lays a finger on yers tell me, I'm not scared of him".

"You think I am?".

"No, I doubt you scare easily," Sean said, smiling. Milly smiled back. She already knew she liked him. This was the most he had talked. It felt like he was letting his guard down.

"Shall we go in?" Asked Mary.

"Yeah come on, we'll get good seats".

They made their way passed the usherette and to the velvet seats facing the stage. To someone who had never been here before, it was a wonderful sight to see. Velvet curtains hung heavily on the stage, lit with oyster shell lights of gold, suited orchestra in the pit, then silence as the lights went down.

Milly held on to Sean's hand, nervous energy flowing through her, Mary watched out the corner of her eye, slightly smiling to herself, they were a perfect match.

The curtains opened and out walked Nelly Pope, glittered leotard with giant pink feathers in her hair and shoes to match. Her big smile and cheeky voice commanded the stage as she sang humorous songs about workmen, shipbuilders and the evil English to riotous laughter. Dancing up and down the stage, Nelly was a 'Great Girl' as the papers put it. For a few bob, you could have the best night of your life here. Her songs made the evils of the time seem frivolous in retrospect.

Milly and Sean laughed together, and it was sealed, they were smitten.

Jimmy and Mary were happy too. It was not often they could afford to go out. They had to be careful. Bombs were still being hidden in the city, not just by Jimmy's crowd but by the Prods as well. The Palace was an easy target. So far, it had been largely ignored.

The curtains went down and Nelly went to her dressing room, the echoes for "encore" ringing in her ears. She loved her fans as much as they loved her.

Chapter 21

The crowds piled out the building in the street, signalling cabs and meandering through to get home.

BANG!!! Came out of nowhere, dust and debris flying. People were screaming! Glass raining down, chaos!

"Catholic Bastards!" and more glass breaking, fire in the streets, people were trampling each other to get away like animals at a slaughterhouse.

"Come on Milly run!" and Sean grabbed her and pulled her through the crowds down an alley. Jimmy and Mary had disappeared in the chaos.

Milly held on like she was permanently fixed to him. They escaped down a dark alley with bins and rats, crowds ran past them, Sean shielded her from them, he really came into his own when he had to be brave.

"Milly you ok, you not injured?". Sean breathing heavily as he held her close, their eyes locking.

"No, I'm fine". She was shaking with fear and confusion.

He looked at her face, red and tearful. She was still beautiful. She closed her eyes and gently kissed him. Suddenly there was no fear or doubt. It was all extinguished.

Jimmy followed shortly after, Mary in tow.

"You two ok, fuckin Prods! Mary you ok? Come on we can't stay here, come on".

They ran through the back streets to get home. Sean held on to Milly as if she was made of diamonds. He was never letting her go.

Running through the streets, screams and shouts, gunshot echoing in the near distance, eyes darting to find a safe haven.

They got to Milly's and she stopped suddenly. Tension rising in her suddenly. Bombs were nothing compared to what her dad would do if he saw Sean.

"What's wrong?" asked Sean.

"We can't go any further, if me da finds out I was with yer he kill us both".

"If he lays a hand on you I'll kill him".

"It's ok I can handle him, he means well, I had a lovely night Sean, I'll be seeing ya".

"Good night Milly". She kissed him on the cheek and dashed home.

She was right. Her dad would kill them both, no doubt about that.

The sound of gunfire and bombs became a regular occurrence in the city so it was nothing to worry about when they were this far away.

Mary knew that Jimmy would leave her soon. The Loyalist rebels were attacking more and more. Lovett would have his work cut out to find out who these were.

"Jimmy, you're going out to that lot you'll get killed" implored Mary.

"Mary, I won't be long, I'm not going there anyway I said I'd meet a few fella's".

"At this time a night?".

"Mary please I'll meet you tomorrow but I have some things I have to do".

"That Briona was right you are wrapped up in it".

Jimmy sighed and turned to her.

"Mary love, Briona is a nobody you shouldn't listen to her, I doubt she would have a lot to say soon anyway".

"What do you mean by that?".

"Mary, don't ask questions you don't want the answer to".

"Jimmy whatever you're wrapped up in just be careful I don't want you coming home in a body bag".

"Don't worry sweetheart I have the luck of the Irish in me" and he kissed her and flew out the door to Sailor-town.

Chapter 22

Lovett raced down to the city, walking through the debris, assessing his city. He was always one step behind and needed to find out quickly who was behind this. It wouldn't be long before he found his man, as with most things, the British Government could pin it on anyone.

O'Hanlon walked to him, book in hand, the dead lying about, their loyalty undetermined.

"Sir, we counted 50 bodies so far, Ms Pope was in the back, she's shook up but not hurt".

"Do we know who is responsible yet?".

"Not yet sir but a witness said it might have been Clarke sir".

"Thomas Clarke?".

"Yes sir".

"Bring him in for questioning", Lovett sighed. He was right, he was always behind, and it was a battle he was losing badly. If Clarke was involved, he had to take him out, but, if he did, the repercussions would be endless, if Clarke was innocent, and Lovett arrested him, there'd be even worse coming. The police were not exactly Belfast's favourite people.

Jimmy walked to Sailor-town, avoiding the watchful eyes, the orange lights illuminating the cobbled streets. Jimmy walked into the house, Colin and No Nose were there.

"Hi lads, Where's Andy?" asked Jimmy in the dimly lit parlour. The candlelight was hiding the slum and its damp walls and bare floors.

"We haven't seen him since yesterday we thought he was with you?".

"I haven't seen him, No Nose, you must know, didn't he go to get Briona?".

"He did, but we haven't seen him since he left the Dockers after kicking out".

"Come on we better go look for him. Did you hear about tonight, they blew the Palace up, fuckin Prod bastards, glass everywhere, I was lucky to escape, I seen Clarkie there, he didn't see me though, he better be careful that Lovett is looking to pin it on someone".

The lads sat silently. In their gut, they knew something had happened to Andy. Either Lovett had got him and they were all done for or, something worse had happened. They all left and began walking the streets, he couldn't have gotten far. The back alleys, endless in their gloom, populated by rats and vermin, escorted the trio. Tall, grimy buildings looming over them.

"Here!" shouted Colin. He knelt, the body cold and blue in the moonlight.

"Oh dear God!" murmured Jimmy, he knelt too, an arm on Colin to steady himself.

"Jesus who did this?" Colin was shocked. Andy was one of them; whoever did this, was stealthy and strong.

"Briona," said Jimmy.

"Surely not, a young woman like that taking out a man no that's wrong".

"Who else then? Look he didn't even fire around" he said examining the gun.

"We gotta move him".

"No, leave him, we'll leave a tip-off, and that's it, we have to distance ourselves from it, pretend we know nothing, then we need to finish the job".

They all stood up heads bowed and said their last goodbyes and sauntered through the alley. Briona was now an even more serious target.

Chapter 23

Milly walked through the house to get her room with as little fuss as possible. Her dad asleep in the chair.

Her tiny footsteps awoken him; he was a drunk but had a hawk-like hearing.

"Milly is that you?" he shouted gruffly.

"Yes dad I'm just getting in, sorry I'm late but there was some awful business at the Palace".

"Aye? What's that's then?".

"Someone threw a bomb in the window, glass and people everywhere".

"And Sean?".

"Sean?" she asked, quietly trying to sound like she had no idea what he meant.

"Yes Sean, I know you went out with him tonight. You know he has a reputation that one".

"Dad! God! No, oh I'm off to bed".

Her dad slowly rose from his chair. Staggering towards her, he went for his belt.

"You'll not see him again, you hear?". His voice loud and venomous.

"Dad, please I will, he's nice" she pleaded.

"He's a Catholic!".

"He's nice!".

"Don't make me mad Milly, you know what will happen!". His eyes were wide with rage.

"Please dad no, I'm old enough to make my own decisions!".

He whipped off his belt and struck her across her tiny body, and she went down, whipping her as she fell, his fury at being defied.

"No daughter of mine will be a Catholic whore ya hear!".

"Dad!" she screamed, covering her head as he whipped her repeatedly. Pulling her hair to hold her in place to confirm his dominance at the end of his buckled belt.

"Get up those stairs and don't come down until you know who's in charge, I'm seeing Father Montgomery tomorrow and you're going to the laundry in Donegal, you'll bring shame on this family!".

Milly stood up crying uncontrollably, as she made her way up the stairs, he kicked her from behind and she stumbled forward, finding it hard to breathe as the kicks rained down, she crawled away and went to her room. Her world was ending. What she had feared was coming true. She would never see Sean again.

Chapter 24

When the city awoke, it was to streets cordoned off, smashed glass and debris littered the roads, sweepers busily trying to get it all up. Lovett sat in his office looking out the window. It was another wet day in Belfast; Autumn was on its way.

O'Hanlon walked in.

"Don't you ever knock lad!".

"Sorry sir, but that girl is here Briona, she's demanding to see you right away".

"Demanding is she! Well can't keep a lady waiting can we" he replied drolly.

"Come on then", and O'Hanlon beckoned. She walked in, dark rings around her eyes and rags for clothes, illustrated her fear.

"Briona, what do we owe this pleasure, more info?".

"Someone tried to kill me last night; someone knows I work for you".

"Oh, Who?".

"How the hell would I know, I need protection".

"Protection? From me, now sure why would I do that".

"Please, I don't want to die, you owe me!".

"Owe you, girl I owe you nothing, you've given me the bare minimum and you were paid we're even".

"Please, they're going to kill me!".

"Who, who is going to kill you?".

"The Titanic lads, they're all part of it, Jimmy sent someone to get me but I got him first".

"You got who first, Briona, have you killed someone?".

"It was self-defence he tried to kill me, please you have to help me, just get me out of here!".

"If you've killed someone Briona the only salvation you'll get is at the end of the rope".

"Screw you I have to go I hope they get you" and she stood to leave, her confession would fall on deaf ears, even if he did believe her another dead Catholic is a good start in his eyes.

Lovett reached into his desk and got out an envelope of money.

"Here, take this and don't let me see you again".

"Jesus, how much is in here?".

"Enough to get you gone, go on get out of here and if you say anything to anyone I'll kill you myself".

She tucked it in her shawl and left. He watched her out the window, disappear in the bodies of grey rags that walked the streets. She turned to look up at him like a dog tossed out on the streets. This was her only chance. Briona had disappeared.

Chapter 25

Milly opened her black eyes to the sunlight peering through the clouds. The house was silent.

She needed to move and quick. Her body racked with pain and bruises, was slow. Bloodstains on her pillow.

Dried tear stains on her face. If Sean saw her, his quiet temperament would explode. It was inevitable.

She put on her clothes delicately and made her way downstairs like a frightened animal. Her dad had left for work already. No doubt he would be back with apologies and promises that this was a one-off and wouldn't happen again.

The wind cooled her beaten face, exposing her injuries that she desperately wanted to hide.

In the distance Mary called, she tried to avoid her, but, Mary being the caring young woman, came running over, at first not noticing that she was being deliberately covert.

"Morning Milly did ya not hear me?".

"Oh sorry, Mary, I didn't hear ya".

"I'm not surprised, why are you hiding your face like that? Oh, I think Sean has it bad for yer".

"Yeah I think he does" she replied, her jaw aching with every word.

"Milly come on I can hardly hear ya", and she turned to see her face. Mary's smile turned to disbelief when she saw the injuries,

"Jaysus Mary and Joseph what happened to you, is this your dads' handy work?".

"I told you he'd go mad if he found out I went out with a Catholic he's sending me to Donegal".

"Donegal?".

"There's a laundry there I can work at".

"You'll not end up going, Wait till Sean sees oh my God".

"No! He mustn't know".

"Well, he's going to see your face".

"He won't cause I'm not seeing him again".

"You can't do that, that's not fair on either of you".

"He wouldn't want to see me any way looking like this, and if my dad does make me leave well then he'll have no choice".

"Come on, let's talk about this later, after work".

They walked into the mill; its tower and windows watching them, the deafening noise of the looms making Belfast's finest lace, working harder than ever. Linens and cloth for the upper classes, beautiful, crisp, stained with the blood of the lower classes who would never own anything so pretty.

The docks were busying themselves, the ship taking form. Higher and higher the men worked without thought for safety.

So far in the last three months, five men had died falling from up on high, one wrong step, and you would be no more.

These were warnings that went unheeded. What other choice did the riveters have? Sam, cocky little man-child that he was, did not seem at all phased by the constant fear that every day may be his last.

He ran too and fro with the rivets in hand, sheet metal being guided into place, his tiny frame in the darkness is easy to miss.

Michael told him time and time again, be careful lad, he wasn't his lad, but, was treated as such, Michael was a caring fellow and would look after anyone in his flock.

"Sam be careful today, we're higher so no messing ya hear me".

"Ok Michael whatever".

"Sam, I'll tell your mammy if you don't listen".

"Tell her I don't care".

"Ya hear that Jimmy he doesn't care".

"He's a braver lad than I then" and they all laughed about. Irish mothers were not to be messed with, and getting the slipper was not a rare occurrence.

Sam ran down and got the rivet from James, he had the best place in these winter months by the hot furnace, if he was quick, he could pilfer a few lumps of coal for his own fire at home, though he had to be careful.

The gangplank, slippery and narrow, was dangerous the higher it went. Sam running up and down it all day, hobnail boots, wearing out, Jimmy watched him coming up with the hot iron, Michael wiping his brow, the boot stuck on the plank, the rivet sailed through the air to the men below, like a flaming ball of lava, in a flash, Sam followed, tiny fingers holding on the sides, Jimmy running to him, leaping on his belly to grab the poor lads arm.

"I'm slipping Jimmy!" cried Sam.

"I got you, pull yourself up" shouted Jimmy holding his sweaty glove.

"Jimmy! Don't let me fall!".

"Michael! Quick!" and he ran down, the vibrations of the men running to their aid, prevented from more help by the cracking of the wood, James watching on in shock, wet hands slipping from their grasp, Sam plummeted hundreds of feet, men watched in slow motion, his body vanishing, plummeting to the dock, hitting it hard. No one would be able to help him. Sam was dead.

"I told him to stop messing about!" cried Michael.

"It's ok, Michael, it's not your fault, it's this bloody ship!" said Jimmy. Sean took off his cap and knelt over his little body. He was a fifteen year old man. Someone laid a blanket over the boy, and a van came and took him away.

The building of the ship stopped for no one. The riveters went back to work.

Chapter 26

Lovett had Clarke in jail. He knew where these guns were, and he needed to know what they were being held for, he wouldn't miss this like he missed the Palace bomb. His reputation was at risk. He was fast becoming known as a man who couldn't get things done.

The cell, dank and grey, hidden from public, held many secrets. It was the last place for many a man accused of treachery against the crown.

Clarke was seated, tethered to a chair, his clothing taken, dirty and bloody from his ill-treatment, he watched silently as Lovett opened the creaking metal door, his heels echoing in the darkness like a clawed beast.

He removed his hat and coat, unbuttoned his waistcoat, he looked like a man about to retire to bed than an interrogation.

Clarke knew his days were coming to an end. An Irish man would not last in English hands. They were a problem. He eyed him with fury and anger.

"Hello Mr Clarke, I've been wanting to talk to you for some time", said Lovett.

Clarke spat in his face. The saliva slowly oozed down Lovett's cheek. It's white silky substance with a hint of blood.

Lovett did not flinch. This was a battle of wills. He wiped away the spit with his white handkerchief, the cleanest item in that cell, it would be grey soon enough.

"Clarke if that's how you want to play it that's fine, I would hope we could talk civilly".

"Talk civilly? That's a laugh, what hope do we have as Irish men to talk civilly when you keep us down, go fuck yourself Lovett I'm telling you nothing".

Lovett knew he wouldn't break easily and that a long night awaited them, he had to find those bombs and prove that Jimmy was involved, Clarke knew he had nothing on him, he'd take his secrets to the grave.

"Tom, may I call you Tom?".

"Call me what you like fucking pig".

"Tom, we need to know where those bombs are going, do you want the blood of Irish men on your hands?".

"Me with the blood, ha, that's rich, how many of us have you and yours gunned down when we fight for our independence".

"Tom, that's not me, I'm one of you, let's just talk and help each other, we can strike a deal, you tell me where those bombs are, and I'll see you escape the last bullet you'll ever see".

"Life in Crumlin? Life in Crumlin may as well be a bullet. You go in there you never come out".

"You can't win this war when you're dead Tom, help us".

"I'm helping the Irish, if my death turns the tide of English Rule then so be it".

"You're not helping anyone sat here".

"Do you know what will happen to me if I become a snitch, I may as well cut me own throat now".

"We'll protect you".

"You, protect an Irish man, that's a laugh".

They sat silently in a great dim cell. It was a stalemate. It was time, time to squeeze.

Lovett rolled up his sleeves. He was done being nice. It was getting him nowhere.

"Tom, I've tried to help you, I've offered you a deal, I've spoken to you nicely, and you've spat in my face and insulted me, you will tell me where those bombs are going and who is planting them, one way or another you will talk, everybody talks in the end. They say try and stay strong, but in the end, they all cry for their mothers. I've seen lads much bigger than you fall to their knees begging for mercy".

"I'll be happy to disappoint you; my mammy is long in the grave".

"Then she'll have company pretty soon" and with that Lovett smashed Clarke in the face with a full fist, his head flew back, his nose exploded into blood and sinew, stinging pain and tears ran down Clarke's face, sight blurred. His glasses smashed. His head down, blood dripping on to his ragged trousers. He shook his head and smiled to himself. He raised his head and eyed up Lovett, he was right, he would be with his mother soon.

"Tell me where the bombs are?!".

"Go fuck yourself!" and a bloody globule of spit hit Lovett in the face. He returned with another smack.

"Is Jimmy Mahon involved?".

"I don't know who that is".

"Sick of this bull shit". Lovett, with his frustration, reaches into his pocket and gets out his knife.

"O'Hanlon get in here!" he yelled and in walked the young officer.

"Hold his fucking hand, Clarke for every time you don't answer me, I'm taking a fucking finger you hear me!".

"Sir, you can't do that!" squirmed the officer, his eyes welling up. He had joined the force to do good, not torture people.

"Shut the fuck up and hold him, Clarke is Jimmy involved?!".

"Fuck you!" he screamed, the knife sawed through the bone of his finger, he was one less as it rolled across the floor.

O'Hanlon felt sick; what had he become? Blood flowed from Clarke.

"Ok ok, please no more," he said breathlessly.

"Finally, is Jimmy involved?".

"Yes, yes he is".

"I knew it, O'Hanlon go bring him in".

"Wait!" said Clarke.

"What?".

"He's involved, with your fucking mother ya English Prick" and Clarke started laughing hysterically.

Lovett looked down, and he had lost all hope that this was going to go well.

"Clarke You are one crazy bastard you know that, come on O'Hanlon, we'll get nothing from him", he wiped his forehead and walked out, leaving Clarke in the chair.

Chapter 27

Clarke sat in the darkness, days of beatings and meagre food barely kept him alive. He didn't tell Lovett anything about the plan. Clarke would die for Ireland and become a martyr.

He opened his eyes, and in the corner stood his mother. Her blue dress and pinny with a cigarette in hand, smiling at him. Her echoey voice calling to him, 'come on son, time to go now'. 'No mammy there's so much more to be done' he replied, 'it's not your fight any more love, come on now you'll see', and she reached for his hand, his pain and tears were gone, the fight wore on without him, the bombs sat idle awaiting their mission.

Chapter 28

It was a long day for all. Milly's face still ached with the bruises. She had done her best to hide from Sean but, as luck would have it, he was coming her way. His face always lit up when she was around. She was his sunlight, his reason for living.

She hid her face from him and tried to avoid his gaze, hoping he wouldn't see her.

"Hey look Sean, Milly, she's avoiding yer" laughed Jimmy.

"Sure, why would she be doing that?".

"Come on, let's go ask her".

"Hey Milly! How's it going, what's up why you avoiding me?".

"I have to go Sean, I can't talk to yer", and she tried to walk away but he grabbed her arm, and she flinched, and tears swam down her blackened face.

"What's wrong Milly tell me" Sean implored, even Jimmy seemed concerned now. She pulled her shawl from her face, and the damage was exposed to gasps and fury.

"Did he do this to ya that piece of shit I'll kill him!", Sean was enraged, a side even Jimmy rarely saw. Mary ran over, trying to catch up Milly.

"Milly why didn't ya wait for me, oh I see you told them".

"Told us what?" asked Jimmy.

"Her da, he's sending her to Donegal, work in the laundries".

"The fuck he is! Milly come to our house".

"I can't he said he kill yer if I see you again".

"Kill me! That drunken sot, come on" and the four walked to Sean's house, he was so enraged even Jimmy was a little intimidated. Sean's mind was running a mile a minute, the short walk home seemed to take forever.

"Sean, I can't go to your house. I have to go I'm sorry" and Milly ran home. She was terrified of what would happen. She walked through the door, and her dad was asleep in the chair, his silver whiskers glistening in the afternoon sun.

She went to the kitchen to make a cup of tea, even walking like a cat he would still hear her, his gruff voice shouting to her.

"Milly, is that you?".

"Yes, dad just making a cup of tea".

"Get in here" he demanded. She sighed, what else could he do to her?

"Yes dad?".

"Come here, right here", and he pointed to the threadbare carpet by his feet, summoning her like a little girl.

"I spoke to Father Montgomery today, he said they would love to take a girl like you, he's going to let me know and then you're off, out this place and from under me feet". Milly stood silent. His threats were usually empty. She died inside. She knew what happened in those places, the abuse, the cruelty.

"No dad!" she implored through streams of tears.

"Don't defy me girl or you'll get more of what I gave yer".

"I'll not go".

"You will go!" and he shuffled to get his belt. In his drunkenness he had no strength and sat there, gasping for air, his stomach from years of heavy ale rising and falling like bellows. His face red and blotched, his blue eyes that were the magnet for the girls were now grey and empty, he had become a ghoul, but, he was still Milly's dad, she would not be going to the laundries for forgotten women. Sean would take care of that.

Chapter 29

Sean, Jimmy and Mary sat in the parlour all quiet, Milly was very close to them, She had no one in the world, and she was the world to Sean.

The fire crackled, breaking the silence.

"Mary, that's not all that happened today".

"Jaysus, what else happened?".

"One of the lads died today, a young un Sam, Michael's still there at the docks, God Mary, you should have seen it, I tried to hold on to him but I just couldn't, he slipped through me fingers".

"Oh Jimmy, that's awful".

Jimmy sighed and a tear swam down his face, Mary kissed his forehead. Sean stared at the fire. Sam's death was a needless tragedy, one of many to happen on that bloody ship, but he could only think of Milly, he couldn't lose her.

Michael walked with the lads to Sam's mothers' house. A visit from the elder dockworkers in the week was never for a positive reason. His mother opened the door.

"Hey, lads what's going on is Sam with yer, he's normally home by now, won't you come in".

Their ashen faces told her something was gravely wrong. They removed their caps and walked in.

"Sit down Mrs Scott, we have some bad news for you", said Michael quietly.

"What is it, where's Sam? Come on now stop ya playing. I'll box his ears if he's in trouble".

"Mrs Scott, Sam died today, he fell from the staging, we're very sorry".

Silence, incredulity, silently begging for it to not be true.

"If this is a joke it's not funny in the slightest, where's my boy?".

"Mrs Scott, it's not a joke, they just took him to the hospital, there was nothing we could do".

Sam was her only son, her husband since passed. Her body trembled with tears and wails of sorrow, heartbreaking into a thousand pieces, Michael put his arm around her, the lads knelt down beside her, there was nothing they could do.

The door knocked heavily and in walked a large lady from the next house, they told her the news, and she stepped forward to comfort the gasping mother in her arms.

The lads stood and left, quietly closing the door. It was not the first or last time they would give bad news about deaths on the ship. It was something they would not get used to.

Chapter 30

Back at the station, Clarke lay on the metal slab overlooked by the mortician. His battered and bruised body, a fallen soldier, stared at the ceiling. Lovett looked at him. He hadn't got the information he needed, and dead ends were multiplying.

That night, the lads were sat in the pub, silent but all were thinking about Milly. Sean stared at his pint. He'd never been so full of fury.

"Sean man will ya just let it go there's nothing you can do about it, you'll make it worse," said Jimmy. He could feel the tension.

"He can't get away with it".

"You'll be straight in Crumlin then you'll never see her again, is that what you want?".

As they sat in the dark corner, Milly's dad stumbled in, paper under his arm, ordering his usual double whisky and a pint. Sean watched him out the corner of his eye and waited.

Sean sat there nursing his drink that grew flatter as the night wore on. The bar emptied and out walked Milly's dad. The lads stood and left also. The streets were bathed in orange light from the lamps, silent, watching.

Milly's dad's steps swayed as he made his way home, the lads just far away enough that he wouldn't hear them stalking him. They sped up to him, their boots echoing on the cobbles.

"Hawey there lads, can I help ya with any tin?" asked Milly's dad.

"Have ya got a light there Paddy?" said Sean, cigarette-less.

"Oh, sure I have here, wait, how do you know my name?". He looked at them suspiciously.

"You don't need to know that" and Sean cracked him in the face and down he went hitting the floor. Sean grabbed him by his collar and belted him in the face over and over, Jimmy, the lookout for any witnesses, this needed to be over.

Sean pulled him up and head-butted him, his drunkenness prevented him from putting up a fight. The gurgling and choking on blood, they dragged him to the docks.

"Jesus Sean, what you doing? Let him go. He's had enough!" begged Jimmy.

"Milly had enough and he didn't stop," Sean snarled.

"You're Sean. You know Milly?! Oh you'll never see her again you fuckin Prole" laughed Paddy.

"I'd stop talking if I was you" implored Jimmy.

They walked him to the docks, his head bobbing, if anyone saw they would think he was drunk.

"Sean, why are we taking him to the docks, just leave him here!" begged Jimmy.

"It doesn't matter, it'll sober him up, God he weighs a fuckin ton", said Sean dragging him under his shoulder.

"This is madness Sean!".

They came to the docks, the waves lapping up the sides and lay him down, his bloody face looking up at them laughing, he crawled to stand.

"You'll never see Milly she's off tomorrow away from you, filthy slut not in my house". His sharp voice even when he was being punched.

"Oh you just don't know when to shut the fuck up".

Sean side punched Paddy and down he went,

"You won't touch her again ya hear me, if ya do I'll kill you meself".

Paddy rolled over attempting to stand, the blows he had received affected his balance, Sean and Jimmy watched as he rolled over the side and into the dark water below, hardly a splash was made and he sank to depths of the Lagan.

"Oh shit Sean quick get him, it's ok beating him but you don't want a murder charge as well", said Jimmy leaning over the side to grab him out of the water.

They scrambled to the floor, reaching in the water to grab him but there was nothing, he sank right down the murky depths.

Jimmy and Sean stood looking at the dark water, silent. Their crime hidden forever.

Sean washed his hands in the water.

"What now then?" asked Jimmy.

"Nothing, we go home and never talk of this, if Milly asks we saw nothing and we know nothing ok, at least she's not going to that place now". Sean sounded stronger than Jimmy had ever seen.

"If she finds out".

"If she finds out, I'd rather go to Crumlin than deal with that," said Jimmy. What had his friend become? The shy lad with a twinkle in his eye had become deranged with anger.

Was it gallant or mindless? Either way, there was no turning back now.

Chapter 31

It was a new day. Sean was a different person now. He stared at the mottled ceiling he wondered how he could look at Milly. Still, he had to work, the world does not stop.

In the office, Lovett was frustrated with the investigation. Where was this bomb and when would it go off. Time was running out. He had to get Jimmy. He knew he had something to do with it.

O'Hanlon walked in, Andy's body had been found and was now in the morgue.

"Briona was right then, that Jimmy, we need to bring him in".

"There's proof it was Jimmy".

"He's mixed up in all this. He'll slip up you wait".

The papers reported Clarke's death, bias against the Irish, reported him to be a criminal rather than a freedom fighter. There would be repercussions that even he could not imagine.

At the docks, the lads were reading the paper.

"Can you believe this horse shit, Clarkes dead, the English bastards shot him they shot him!" said Colin angrily.

There was a quiet in Belfast, one of their own was now gone, the leader of the war against Home Rule, it wouldn't stand and only added fuel to the fire.

Colin and No Nose walked to the docks, unaware of the events. The beautiful sunlit day was about to become the start of a dark and bomb filled era.

"Morning Michael," said Jimmy, he was not his usual jubilant self.

"Sure, what's up with you lad, you and Mary had a fight?".

"No, no just tired is all, had a late drink last night".

"Ahhh a hangover, you know how to cure a hangover, more drink" laughed Michael.

"I'm sure we can hammer a million rivets on a few pints of grog".

"Say where's Sean he's never late, probably shacked up with one his girlfriends".

"Aye probably" Jimmy looking at nothing, his mind elsewhere. He wasn't a virgin to violence, but Sean was like a brother to him, he worried for him. He wasn't the sort to fight let alone kill someone. Sean was walking to work slowly, feeling eyes upon him. He had to shake it off. Only he and Jimmy knew what had happened and he could trust him with his life, but still, the paranoia crept in.

"Jimmy, when you gonna be asking Mary to marry ya, it's about time you got married at your age and Mary isn't getting any younger".

Jimmy laughed; the change in subject to the love of his life was a welcome one.

"Do you think she'd say yes?".

"All women say yes Jimmy unless you want sex then it's usually no" Michael giving a throaty wheezed laugh.

"Oh Mick, that's your daughter, you shoudn't talk like that".

"Ah so, you gonna ask her then?".

"I'll think about it".

"She's a great girl you'll find no one better. She's got fire that one".

"That she has, anyway come on we be late".

They walked in and Colin was waiting for them, puffing away on his roll-up.

"Jimmy, Michael, have ya read the papers this morning?!".

"God, what's up with u, no we not read the papers why ya horse come in or something?".

"Oh my God, Clarke he was put up the wall! They shot him. They shot him".

"They shot him? Who shot him?".

"They said he was an enemy of the state committing crimes against the Crown".

"Michael I've got to go I'll catch up to ya in a minute".

"I made the tip, they must have Andy by now, that Briona, haven't seen her in a while, she must be in hiding".

"Hopefully it's scared her to be quiet," said Jimmy.

"It better had. I can't believe he's gone" sighed Colin.

"There's no point crying about it now. We need to go to the Dockers tonight see Seamus move those guns".

"Ok I'll see you there," said Colin, and he walked to his station.

Men came and went at the docks, and if a man didn't turn up, his vacancy was quickly filled.

Upon the scaffold, the hammering and sparks reigned, rivets hammered in, the ship body coming together.

Michael had burning questions for his prospective son in law, but he thought better of it. Sometimes it's best not to know. Burning questions desperate to free themselves; he shook his head to get them away from his lips. You shouldn't ask questions you don't want the answer to.

Chapter 31

The sun stroked Milly's face awake. The house was unusually quiet.

Normally woken to Paddy shouting her for a cup of tea, but there

was nothing, not a sound. Only the noise of the docks in the distance

floating on the air.

She got dressed and made her way downstairs, called out his name

but nothing. She checked his bedroom, empty bottles lying about his

bed dishevelled but the bed was cold, he had not returned home. He

would always make it back, she thought. As much as she hated him,

she needed him. She had an ominous feeling. After ordering her to

pack to go to the laundry, she felt like this was a dream, and she

wouldn't be going, that she knew for sure.

She opened the front door and saw her neighbour beating the carpet

on the step.

"Say misses you seen me da this morning?".

"No love, did he not come home?".

"No, his beds not been slept in".

"Ah he's probably sleeping it off somewhere I shouldn't worry men

always come back for their tea".

"I guess, thanks anyways, I best be going". Milly shut the door and walked the cobbled streets to the mill, wondering if something terrible had happened.

Mary caught her up, wrapped in her shawl, Milly always made her smile, so meek and innocent, and that rat for a father, Mary's temper would be a match for him if he were her father.

"Milly, you're awful quiet this morning".

"Da never came home last night. He always makes it back after a few, even when it's a few too many".

"Would it be so bad if he didn't?".

"Mary! He's still me da, oh I hope nothing happened to him".

"Would serve him right if it did, after what he did to you".

"It's not him it's the drink, when he's sober, when he was sober he was lovely, God what if something happened what'll I do?" Milly said with a croak trying to hold back tears of panic.

"You'll live the life you want and be free from his fists is what you'll do".

They made their way to the awaiting whirring machines, the dust off the lace flooding their lungs like a fog of cotton, pulling the looms this way and that, folding the linen and wiping their brow. Men always say women's work like they are less than they are, but work is work, and no work is easy when you're poor.

The lads made their way to Sailor-town, the run-down little streets, gaslights flickering on tatty wooden doors to tatty little hovels. They walked in and sat with the residents and hatched their plan.

"Ok so I have the guns hidden we can pick them up no one else knows they're there, when the governors are all in we can take them all out, any trouble we'll make them pay for what they did to Clarke".

"When are we going to strike?".

"A couple of weeks, any longer it won't mean anything, they need to know that we are not a weak nation, this is for Ireland. Colin, you and No Nose keep watch, see who goes in and out, I'll get the guns with Davey, and you two go set the bomb up".

"Aye, we'll put it by the entrance when they're all in, if any come out we can shoot there heads off like they did with Clarke".

The mini-army each drank a whiskey and departed. Davey and Jimmy drove into the darkness, it was late and the city was quiet. The canals were empty at this time of night. Even the vagrants were asleep. Moving barrels and crates the guns were loaded and ready to be transported to Sailor-town. A street of the lowest classes had no scruples for a quick Punt, it was easy work, and they had a common goal, Ireland.

Chapter 33

The next day Jimmy had decided, tonight he would take out Mary
and ask her to marry him. He didn't see a better time for it and who
knows what the future would bring. There was a show on he could
take her to, it would be perfect, her dad was right, there's no other
like her and someone like her wouldn't wait forever.

Walking to work, his mind focussing on how he was going to ask
kept his mind off his plans.

To the English he was a terrorist, to the Irish, he would be a hero.
Even if he failed, at least he would have done something. Lovett
was waiting for him.

O'Hanlon walked into his office, he didn't have much news but what
he had was valuable enough.

"Sir the guns, I don't know where they are but Jimmy is planning
something, one of the drunks said he saw him moving crates at the
canal at night, why would you do that if you're not hiding
something, I think we should bring him in for questioning".

"One of the drunks? Which one?".

"Charlie Evans sir said he saw him".

Lovett sighed. He had to make a move. He was stuck.

"Go get him, take one of the others with you I doubt someone like that will come quietly. Even if we don't get anything out of him, it'll shit him up and then we can just watch". O'Hanlon left to get Jimmy.

The lads tinkered away at the Ship Of Dreams, her body coming together on time. Thoughts of revolution in everyone's minds. Except for Michael, he was desperate to get Mary married to Jimmy, it was a difficult time in Ireland, and he knew that Jimmy was up to something but, he treated him as a son and could forgive his indiscretions.

"So Jimmy, are ya gonna ask her then?".

Jimmy didn't answer, but the smirk on his face gave him away. The hammering carried on and then their ears pricked up. Through the noise of the yard, a message was being hammered like Morse code. The police were looking for Jimmy. He looked down, and Bourne and O'Hanlon were looking up at him beckoning to come down. Time had suddenly stopped. Were they coming to ask about the body, the guns or his associates? The best thing to do was to keep his mouth shut. He sighed and dropped his hammer.

"Sean take over will ye, I think I have a visitor".

Sean looked down, his heart sank. They must have found the body.

"Jimmy! Oh my God, they must have found him".

"They can't have, just keep ya mouth shut, I'll handle it," said

Jimmy, he was stronger in mind than Sean. Sean would confess to

anything given the chance, guilty or not.

Jimmy made his way down the platform wiping his black hands on

his even blacker breeches, eyes watching as he went.

"Yes, Officer, can I help you?" he said innocently as he could.

"Jimmy Mahon?".

"At your service".

"Could you come with me to the station we want to have a chat".

"Well, I'm kinda busy, you know, see the ship?". He said

sarcastically.

"Jimmy don't be smart she still be here for ya when you get back,"

said Bourne, he was suspicious of Jimmy and disliked him since the

day he started. Bloody catholic, can't trust them, would serve him

right if he ended up on the gallows he thought.

"Right you are".

The duo walked to the van and in he got. The dark cage with its wooden seat, the door slammed shut, and the slow drive to the station left him with his thoughts. As brave as he was, he had nervous energy, he kept it inside, say nothing to no-one about anything, they don't know anything.

Chapter 34

The station, Victorian brick and wooden reception, loud prisoners waiting to be seen and assessed, greeted the pair. Jimmy took a seat, and O'Hanlon went to Lovett. Through the blinds, Jimmy could see they were talking but could not make out the muffled words. Lovett stood, tidied himself up and walked out.

"So Jimmy Mahon we meet at last", puffing his chest out. It was true. He knew nothing really of any use, Clarke had given him nothing, Jimmy knew something and Lovett's arrogance would prove useless too. Jimmy was smart. He was his nemesis. He beckoned him in like a schoolmaster with two fingers and in he walked.

"Take a seat. You want a drink?" asked Lovett pouring a whiskey at the oak cabinet.

"Sure why not".

"Only the finest in here son".

The golden-brown whiskey, Irelands finest glistened in the sun as it sloshed on the table.

"I suppose you didn't just bring me here for a drink".

"No, you're right, I suppose you read about Clarke".

"I did".

Jimmy's blood was beginning to boil. His comrade shot, or so he believed.

"Terrible business. How's the ship coming along?".

"Beautifully sir, she'll be the jewel of Ireland".

"That she will I'm sure. Call me John".

"Ok John, can we hurry this up I have to go back to work".

"A hard-working man I see, honest worker".

"That I am sir, John" Jimmy taking a sip from the devil's cup. It was a battle of wills. He'd be getting nothing from me he thought.

"Ok I'll get to the point. There's a rumour going around that something big is going to happen in Belfast, you wouldn't know anything about that, would you?".

"Big?", their eyes meeting, trying to read each other. Jimmy sat back in his chair, relaxed. He reached into his pocket for a smoke, a small act of defiance.

"Yes, we have had intelligence that some guns came into the city via your yard".

"I wouldn't know about that. I'm just a riveter, try the Protestants".

"The Protestants?" Lovett chuckled under his breath. He looked out the window smiling. This would be harder than he thought.

"Yeah filthy English loving bastards, I wouldn't trust em".

"Would you not?

Well maybe I'll look into that. What do you know about Briona Duffy?".

"Can't say I've heard of her".

"Oh? That's strange, she works with your Mary, and you've never heard of her?".

"Mary has a lot of friends I can't keep up".

"So you don't know her?".

"No, like I said, Mary has a lot of friends".

"She told us that you hid guns in a bar, The Dockers Rest".

"Did she now? I wouldn't know anything about that. You'd have to go see yourself, I only drink in there".

"You only drink there. Course you do. Why do you think she would say your name specifically out of all the men that go in there?".

"I wouldn't know, you'd have to ask her, maybe she's jealous of Mary and me".

"Women can be jealous I'll give you that, hell hath no fury and all that".

"More vicious than a sewer rat when they have a mind to".

"If I bring Mary in, I reckon she knows something you're not telling me. I can be very persuasive".

Mentioning Mary made Jimmy roar internally. No one goes after his Mary. His brow furrowed, and he placed his glass on the table. He leant forward.

"I wouldn't do that if I was you".

The mood suddenly turned hostile.

"And whys that may I ask?".

"She doesn't know anything, and I'm warning you,

you go after her I'll go after you, and no English crown will save you".

"Are you threatening a Chief Inspector son?".

"No, I'm telling ya, you've got nothing on me, and I'm going".

"You'll go when I say you can go and I know you know more. I'll lock you up for obstructing the law".

"I've answered your questions, and now I'm going". Jimmy was right. They had nothing on him. They could search the pub all they want. He was one step ahead. Jimmy walked out.

"I'll be watching you, Jimmy, I'll get ya eventually fucking Fenian bastard".

Jimmy walked out coolly. Fuming that Mary would be bought in. It's right she knew nothing but her suspicions would be his downfall. Lovett stood at the window, watching Jimmy walk back to the dock. He necked his whiskey and threw the glass at the wall in frustration. He was no closer now than when he started.

He had to play it carefully. He didn't want a raid that would lead to a riot, but he had to strike. He had to go to Sailor-town. There he would find the answers.

Chapter 35

Jimmy walked through the yard gates, eyes watching him. Colin gave a secret nod, Jimmy replied with a bobbing head, they had to meet. No Nose watched from his station. He would get word to the others; the time to strike was fast approaching.

The short day felt longer with the waiting to go home; Jimmy had to hurry. He had to see Mary.

"Ah Jimmy Mary be waiting for ya there's no rush," said Michael unaware of the events. The lads walked back. Sean desperate for answers.

"Jimmy so what happened?".

"Don't worry. It's not about you. Keep your mouth shut", and Jimmy sped walked to Mary's house. Mary was inside making tea as usual, humming a tune to herself, she was in love with Jimmy and longed for the day for him to marry her, but her strong will would never let on. When he walked in, her heart skipped like a teenager, but her manner belied her age. The tough times of being a working-class girl, working since she was 11, she had been an adult more than a child, and it had given her an old head on young shoulders.

"Afternoon Jimmy, Da you want a cuppa tea I'm just making one".

"Be nice thanks love" he said, slumped into his chair. Wiping his brow with his cap, days got harder for him as he aged. He looked at Jimmy smiling. He knew what was coming.

"Say Mary, would you like to go to the picture house tonight, my treat?".

"Tonight?".

"Yes, unless you have a better offer".

"I might have better offers but let's see what you have" she laughed.

"I'll pick you up at 7 Mary. I gotta go, see ya, Michael". Jimmy dashed out the door.

"See ya son".

Mary sat at the table, pouring the tea, wondering about his urgency.

"Well, that boy always surprises me, I'll never work him out, what you smiling for Da did I miss something?".

"Oh no, no not really, just something funny I heard".

"Well, don't keep us all waiting," said Ma.

"It's ok, I'll tell ye later".

Mary looked at him, suspiciously. He knew something alright. All would be clear later on.

Milly walked into the quiet house, her da still not returned. It wasn't the first time he had up and left for days, not a word. Hopefully, this was it. She walked to the dock, but they hadn't seen him either. He wouldn't get paid if he didn't show up, and Milly's meagre allowance would see her evicted soon. She sat in the parlour, the ticking clock for company as she sipped her tea. Though she wanted to be free of him, she needed him. When he did get back, she would let him have it, although she knew she wouldn't if she didn't want a clout. She learnt that from a young age. She stopped hiding the bruises. It was pointless as new ones would just show up.

Davey and Colin made their way to the house, careful not to be watched. No Nose was carrying the rear.

If you didn't know him you'd never see him, his small stature and dark face from the furnaces made him the perfect lookout.

The duo walked in and sat down. The bomb makers were sitting casually. "What's up lads?" said Colin.

"Jimmy was collared today. By Lovett. He said he doesn't know anything, but I think we're being watched. Jimmy be here soon" said one of the bomb makers. Nameless engineers who would be the best in Belfast.

"Did Jimmy say anything?" asked Colin.

"No, of course not why would he?" replied Davey.

"We have to be careful who we trust".

"You can trust Jimmy, feck's sake. When he gets here, he tell ya all about it". The silence was heavy, and suspicions of each other grew, they had to keep it together, to divide would be their downfall, it's what the English want. A tap at the window from No Nose indicated a visitor; it was Jimmy. He walked in coolly puffing on a woodbine. No Nose waited outside, looking inconspicuous. He could find more information than the government about anything, he'd make a terrific spy, but his sullen brain though it held the information he knew not what to do with it. He was perfect for confession, you could tell him, but he wouldn't understand really, and he was a friend for life.

"Lads, did Davey tell ya?" asked Jimmy.

"Yeah, what did you say to him?" Colin worried.

"I said nothing, he doesn't know anything, he asked me about Briona, has anyone seen her?".

"No, not in a long time," said Davey.

"He said he's going to talk to Mary".

"Oh great she'll have us all up the wall" cried Colin.

"She won't, she doesn't know anything either, we gotta move quick, I have to talk to Mary first then we can set things up, just keep ya mouths shut and watch out for him, there's an officer named O'Hanlon, I don't think he's on Lovett's side".

"What makes you say that, he's a peeler loyal to the crown," said Colin.

"I don't think he is, it was a feeling I got, he could have knackered me when he wanted, but he didn't, he was polite, he might be able to help us, I'll get No Nose on it, see if he can find anything out, I've seen him in the Rest, I gotta go, tomorrow lads, after the service, we'll go to the Rest see if he's there".

Jimmy walked out and had muffled words with No Nose, and he sauntered off. He had no urgency that one, Jimmy made his way to the theatre for the show, tonight would be the start of his new life. And maybe the end.

Chapter 36

The night air was fresh and smelled of stale beer, and the lights glistened on the theatre. Jimmy was nervous for the first time in his life. Mary was the love of his life, and he had no doubts she would say yes. Mary was rounding the corner. Her red hair flowing behind her, she was a vision. Her innocence drew her to him, she had her suspicions about the things he got up to, but she didn't think about it. He was a good man, and she could do a lot worse.

She put her hands around his eyes, playfully, "Guess who" she giggled.

"If it's not Mary I'm going to be real upset" he replied smiling. He turned around and looked at her face. Her blue eyes were staring back at him. He kissed her and grabbed her hand, and they walked in a bustling crowd and grabbed a drink from the bar.

"You look nervous, Jimmy, you ok?" Mary asked.

"Yeah, I'm fine, you look beautiful tonight, Mary".

"Oh thanks, such a rush to get ready, what made you want to go out so suddenly, is Sean with ya?".

"No, it's just us".

"I haven't seen him in a while, Milly's dad still not come home, I do worry about her".

"I'm sure he'll turn up, like a bad penny".

For a few minutes felt like hours in their silence.

"Mary you and me we've been together for a while now, I think we're great".

"Oh, you do?" Mary replied, coyly looking at her drink.

"I love you, I think you love me though you never say it", he held her hand, looking at her like she was a work of art. He could look at her all day, the lines in her face, her red lips, most beautiful.

"I do love you, Jimmy", she kissed his soft lips.

"So I want to ask you something".

"Oh?". Mary looking up at him, her eyes searching trying to work him out.

"Mary would ya marry me?", breathless and his heart racing, he was not afraid of what most Irish men feared, but with her, she made him fearful, he couldn't live without her. She was the better half of him; without her, he was nothing. She sat silently, torturing him. A smile drew across her blushed face. She sighed as if thinking of the answer, but she already knew.

"Yes. Yes, I'll marry ya" she beamed.

"Oh Mary, you made me the happiest man in the world", they kissed, and in his pocket, he reached for the ring. A small gold ring with a little gem of amethyst, it fitted perfectly as it slid on to her finger. She wrapped her arms around him, and it was as if it was made in heaven, they kissed and smiled.

"It was me grandmothers".

"It's beautiful. Oh I can't believe it Jimmy Mahon wants to marry me". Holding her hand up examining her adorned finger, the gems sparkling in the light.

"I do Mary", and he raised his glass and announced it to the world and everyone cheered, raised a glass to him and some clapped, others looked around at the smiling couple.

They finished their drinks and went to the show hand in hand. This was so perfect. Nothing would spoil tonight.

The songs sang on stage, and the dancing flew by, they walked home. It had happened so quickly. It was as if butterflies had carried them home.

They walked in, and her parents were waiting up smiling, Michael couldn't keep a secret even if his life depended on it. The table laid with drinks.

"Ma Da, we getting married!" exclaimed Mary. They engulfed her in hugs and Jimmy handshakes.

"Welcome to the family Jimmy son, Oh we so happy for ya finally" Ma and Da smiling and full of joy.

"Aye thanks Michael, let's have a drink", and it flowed into the early hours.

"Mary we'll have to set a date soon ya know in case ya change ya mind" he laughed.

"I won't change me mind Jimmy, you best go though, I'll see ya tomorrow".

They kissed and all retired for the evening though no one slept for the excitement.

Jimmy walked home through the dark streets; he had almost forgotten about his plan.

Chapter 37

Church the next day was a devil to wake up to. The liquor from the previous evening had made the lads struggling to listen to the sermon.

Father Patterson, portly and red from the communion wine held on to the lectern like it was a life raft as he mumbled on about peace times. A random hiccup interrupted to giggles from the congregation, whispers of him drinking the holy-father and giggles from the children as mothers nudged them to behave.

The crowd walked out to the sunlight and to the pub while the women went home to prepare the dinners for the men when they returned.

Jimmy met the lads at the Dockers Rest to further their plan.

"So lads I have sometin to tell ye, I'm marrying Mary" smiled Jimmy to the cheer of his crew, they raised a toast to him and Mary, it was a beautiful piece of news in such harsh times.

"So Jimmy, you set a date yet?".

"No, not yet, have you seen Sean I thought he'd be here I haven't seen him about".

"No not seen him, maybe he's with Milly".

"Maybe".

"He's acting awful strange lately that one, I saw him the other day just looking at the water, miles away he was, I called him, and he didn't even look up".

Jimmy began to get the feeling again that something terrible had happened to him. A brother from another mother.

"I'll pop by later see how he's getting on, any way lads I'm getting married!" to the cheer and raised glasses. "I'll get a round in" to more cheers.

Jimmy saw O'Hanlon sitting at the bar. It was hard to recognise him out of uniform. You wouldn't know he was the police unless you knew him. He said nothing to him as he supped his beer. Jimmy was right. He may have been the Royal Irish, but he was on their side. He knew that Lovett was corrupt; it wasn't why he had joined. He wanted to protect Ireland not kill it. Jimmy came over and sat by him.

"I don't see you here often," said Jimmy, not making eye contact.

"I don't always come here, what do you want Jimmy I can't be seen talking to you".

"Just keep looking at your pint, and nothing will happen. Tell me what you know about Lovett".

"What I know? You already know, he's watching you, and your lads".

"The mans a fool. Couldn't catch a cold that one".

"He already took one of you out; you think he won't do that to you" O'Hanlon regretted saying that, he let on too much.

"Yeah had Clarke shot. You kill one of ours makes us stronger".

"Jimmy, I believe in a free Ireland, but it's never gonna happen you should quit this before you end up the wall".

"Like Clarke?".

"Clarke didn't get shot Jimmy".

Silence.

"What do you mean?".

O'Hanlon sighed and drank. Rubbed his face, his confession and honesty, Jimmy knew was one of theirs.

"He bought Clarke in to rat you out but Clarke said nothing, Lovett, he killed him".

"Yeah he shot him".

"No Jimmy! He beat him to death! He left him in the cell bleeding to death and he died".

Jimmy was stared at the optics on the back wall, rage filling him ready to explode. But he couldn't. He had to keep it in lest everyone knew.

"I gotta go Jimmy, just watch out ok, I said nothing, I'm on your side, but I'm the law I can't protect ya".

"You go, we won't come after you", still looking at the optics.

O'Hanlon disappeared into the Sunday crowd and Jimmy sat motionless. Shocked and unthinking, his mind racing, this news had spurred him on in his mission.

The lads walked to him and sat at the bar.

"So what did he say?" enquired Colin.

Silence.

Davey shook him and looked at Colin and No Nose.

"Clarke, he wasn't shot. They beat him to death. They fucking murdered him the bastards".

"Oh shit" whispered Davey.

"I'm gonna fucking kill him. That's fucking it, to Ireland".

They all raised a glass and made their way to Sailor-town. The plan now set in motion.

Chapter 38

The lads made their way to the house. No Nose trailing.

"It's time. We do it Friday 11 o clock, they be in for their meetings then, throw the bomb in and as they come out we shoot whoever moves, you get the guns and tell the others to be ready, I'm going to look out for Lovett, he won't be there chicken shit bastard won't be anywhere near it".

"What about that O'Hanlon? He'll grass for sure".

"He won't, he said he's on our side and that Lovett is looking for me, he don't know about you lot, there'll be a van parked up, wait there, when you hear the bomb go jump out and you know what to do. We won't get out of this, there's no Crumlin for us. We die for Ireland!".

"For Ireland!". And the plan was set.

Jimmy walked to Sean's house, the curtains were closed and it all looked very quiet. He knocked on the door and no answer. Looking up, he saw the curtain twitch.

"Come on Sean I know you're in open the door will ye" Jimmy bellowed.

The lock turned, and the door opened to a dark living room. Sean sauntered off.

"Sean, where you been we all missed ya down the pub I have great news".

"Oh?". Not looking at him. He was in a world of his own.

"Yeah me and Mary we getting married, you can be me best man".

"Congratulations Jimmy, I'm happy for ya".

"You don't sound happy, why is it so dark in here, come on let me open these curtains", Sean slumped in a chair.

"Jimmy, I'm hiding".

"Hiding? From what, you got a girl after ya again you old dog" he laughed.

"No Jimmy I'm serious, they'll find him then come for me".

"Oh for feck's sake Sean will ya forget it already they won't, and if they do they won't tie it to you, doing this they will get suspicious just snap out of it, come on have a drink wimme I'm getting married".

Sean blinked at the sunlight, Jimmy was right and his best friend , he knew he wouldn't allow anything to happen to him. He rose from his tattered chair and grabbed two glasses and a bottle. The Irish would always have some whiskey in the house.

"There you go lad, see Jimmy fix you right up, have you seen Milly at all?".

"No, nothing ".

"You should go see her, I bet she misses ya, just don't say anything about you know what though, it'll benefit no one".

"How can I look her in the face after what I did".

"Look her in the face? You saved her life, that Paddy was a wrong un and if you hadn't have done it she'd be God knows where now, you did her a favour".

"That is true".

"He'd have drank himself to death, and besides he had a lot of enemies in this town if you hadn't done it someone else would have".

They drank their whiskey and Sean began to feel better.

"Sean, I best be going, get washed up I'll see ya tomorrow, ok".

"Ok, Jimmy. I'll be seeing ya".

Jimmy left and felt better that Sean was marginally ok. He was right though, Paddy had a lot of enemies, usually from gambling debts or fights he had started. Sean had nothing to worry about; the only thing that would let him down would be his conscience that would leak from his mouth.

Sean sat in the sunlight, his mind filled with guilt but also that he had done the right thing, He would do anything for Milly and was envious that Jimmy was marrying the love of his life. He knew he and Milly were star crossed; there was always a glimmer of hope that they would unite. He could either confess all and she would love him for saving her, or he could not tell her and marry her and be guilty forever, then if she found out, well, she would probably kill him herself.

Chapter 39

Monday. It was not only the start of a new week, the beginning of a new life. The lads, including Sean, made their way to the dock, crowds of men and women grabbing their time boards and walking up the scaffold. One would think you would run out of rivets, but there were still millions to go. Davey, Colin and No Nose nodded from their stations, faces already blackened, the furnaces being put in place. So big you could fit an army in there, 159 of them big bastards in this ship, some were bigger than the hovels that the poor lived in, though they weren't much cleaner. Men would shovel coal into them to keep her moving; they were the first to die on that fateful night. As the water rose, the oven hissed as the temperature dropped from the Atlantic ocean. They were a sight to be seen; everything about Titanic was enormous, including the purses of the rich that sailed on her. No expense was spared. The finest linen, the darkest oak, teak and pine, it was a floating heaven, for the rich. Not the poor though. They still had the very basics, one toilet for them and it was on a different deck, shared between them all, they were treated as less than nothing and they had built the damn thing.

The team were hammering away, the water lapping at the side the hills in the distance green and beautiful.

There was a commotion down the side of the dock. Jimmy looked down. He wasn't afraid of heights. You couldn't be in this job if you were. One false step and you'd be closer to the floor than you wished. He looked at Sean, his eyes telling his worse fears. They all got up and watched as a blue, bloated body was fished out and dragged to the dock.

It wasn't a pretty sight. They removed the weeds and debris from his sunken face, eyes staring up at them. Skin like tissue paper, his lips peeled back to give a toothy grin, surrounded by the men, shouting for help. Bourne charging through, no one stops work unless he says. "Probably another pisshead, come on let me through, move it!" The crowd opened up.

"Oh dear lord! Call an ambulance!" he exclaimed.

"He don't need an ambulance he needs a priest" laughed one. A cold look glared at the crowd.

"Cover him up, no one touch the body, shit! Oh Jesus, move it get an ambulance, lads, get back to work", Bourne was panicking, another death at his yard, this time it wasn't his fault.

"Who is it? Anyone from here?" asked Mr Quint.

"I don't know him, probably a drunk" murmured Bourne.

"It's Paddy McCaffery," said a lone voice.

"Who?".

"Paddy, he goes in the Dockers Rest, piece of work he is, wouldn't surprise me if he was drunk", the voice, a faceless man in the crowd, a regular at the pub.

The crowd dispersed as the ambulance arrived. They loaded the body into a bag and took him away.

"Jimmy" whispered Sean.

"It's ok it's just another fallen off the top more like," said Jimmy trying to reassure him, he knew who it was, but he couldn't have him losing it right now.

Sean sighed, he was a loose cannon, that's why Jimmy never lets him know about his plans. He's not a snitch, but he wasn't a bright spark where secrets needed to be kept.

Echoing through, Bourne was shouting everyone get back to work, and the crowds dispersed, the body was taken away, and everyone went back to work. The yard was a dangerous place, and yes men died there daily, they were replaceable in these hard times.

Jimmy could see that Sean's mind was elsewhere.

At the mill word soon got around, they found a body, Milly's dad.

Milly so far was unaware.

Mary was outside smoking with Milly.

"Milly I got something to tell ye".

"Oh what's that then?".

 "Jimmy asked me to marry him, look" and she showed her the ring.

"Oh Mary, that's grand, I'm so happy for ya, hey you're not caught are ya?".

 "Oh go on no I'm not, would ya be me bridesmaid?".

 "Like you have to ask, of course, I will, have you set a date yet?".

 "No maybe next spring".

"A spring wedding it'll be beautiful. Are your Ma and Da happy?".

 "Yeah they're over the moon, finally something to look forward to eh?".

 "Yeah be nice".

"They still not found ya Da yet?".

"No, they said cause he gone before and come back that's probably what he'll do, Mary what if I lose my home?".

"You can live with us; there's room, don't worry".

"Maybe".

"Or you could live with Sean" laughed Mary.

"Ha go on with ya" said Milly laughing through the smoke.

"He'd love that, treat you like a princess that one, you been seeing him a while now".

"Oh, but to live in sin".

"Well, you could get married".

"It took him how many years to ask me out it'd be the rapture before he asked for my hand".

"That it will be".

The ladies threw their butts on the floor and made their way to the looms. In the offices above them, there was a commotion, and Mr Dryden was looking down rubbing his face. He had grave news.

He walked down the metal stairs to the floor and made his way to Milly and Mary. The girls at the other looms watched as he approached. Milly busily folding the linen didn't notice him coming. Mary nudged her. She turned and for a second couldn't think what it would be about, for a second she was still happy.

"Milly, I have some news, about your dad".

Milly stood silently, a premature tear running down her face. Mary put her arm around her and looked earnestly hoping for good news, but this was in vain.

"Mary, you best come up too". They walked to the office, everyone looking up, trying to read the situation, Milly rocked back and forth in Mary's arms, and they closed the blinds to prying eyes.

The office door opened and the ladies walked slowly down the stairs, Dryden, though a tough man to work for, was fair when he had to be and told them to go home. Milly, ashen and silently walking as if in a trance was taken home by Mary.

One pain had ended another had begun.

Chapter 40

At the station Lovett had heard of the death, he had spoken to Milly about her missing dad but had dismissed her, he was a drunk Irish man who had a wandering eye, why waste precious time looking for him.

He made his way to the morgue; an autopsy must be done in these circumstances, it had to be determined if was it the drink or something else that killed him.

The bright white lights reflected on the tiled walls, ahead of him lay the body on a metal slab, lifeless eyes staring at the ceiling. Dr Brown was preparing for the procedure, latex gloves at the ready.

The smell hit you as soon as you entered. A pond-like smell with rotting meat in the background.

Lovett hovered before coming in. He wasn't scared of bodies, he'd seen enough death in the line of duty, but not this close up and not this decayed.

"Mr Lovett a pleasure" Dr Brown extended his brown gloved hand, Lovett looked at it and declined to shake it, Brown smirked.

"We have Paddy McCaffrey then," said Brown looking at a clipboard.

"Yes, not a pretty sight as you can see".

"Drowned in the Lagan by all accounts, the town drunk, 45 years old".

"I can't tell if he drowned until I open him up, if there's water on the lungs he drowned, if not he still may have drowned, but the alcohol content will let me know the answer, if you want to watch there's a gown over there", gesturing to the wall of white gowns. It was a horror story in there. Big metal doors holding rows of bodies waiting to be dissected for various investigations and whatnot.

Lovett hung his jacket and felt confident at this point, having got used to seeing only the head.

"Nervous Lovett?" asked Brown smiling.

"No, not at all! Nothing bothers me I've seen it all" trying to look unnerved.

"Ah, very good, then shall we begin?". Brown was a joker. He could spot the fakes a mile away, the fainters, the ones who throw up, the starers. It was a game he liked to play with himself. He was always right. He'd been playing it too long.

The sheet was pulled back to reveal the naked, part skinless body. Detritus from the seafloor dotted around the corpse, Lovett desperately trying to look masculine and hiding his revolt.

"Subject is male, roughly five feet seven weighing 190 pounds, we removed his clothes, we'll look at those later. No visible signs of foul play, bruising to the face and torso, possibly caused by the fall in the water. Loss of fingernails tells me he's been in the water some time. Eyes clouded over, skin loose, he's been down there a while then say three weeks, time to open him up. Still with us Lovett?" asked Brown not looking up. He reached for the scalpel and began.

Lovett watched as the cuts were made. The skin peeled back like an orange, tissue-thin, Lovett heaved.

"If you need water there's a tap over there," said Brown not looking up.

"I'm fine," Lovett said coughing to hold back his sick. The smell was pungent as the rib cage exposed.

"Looks like a Sunday Lamb shank don't ya think" smiled Brown.

"Oh dear lord" grimaced Lovett. He wouldn't eat meat again after this.

"Nonsense man, pull yourself together, think of it as the Sunday roast being carved. Shall we carry on" he said sarcastically.

"Please do". Holding a hanky to mouth and nose.

"Ok, rib spreader please," he asked his assistant.

The ribs cracked open like eggshells revealing the lungs, stomach and intestines. He reached in and pulled out the lungs and weighed them.

"One point seven kilograms, let's see if they have water in them?".

Brown inserted a plastic tube into the base of the lung and a trickle of water leaked out into a beaker below.

Lovett heaved again.

"You know, I can come and tell you what I have found instead of you standing there heaving like a child".

Lovett took a deep breath and left. Brown smiled to himself.

Lovett made his way to his office as pale as the body he just abandoned to science and slumped in his chair. Trembling, he grabbed his whiskey and poured a double-double and knocked it back. Post mortems were definitely not for him.

Chapter 41

Milly sat with Mary having tea. The world seemed quiet to her now; at least she knew he wasn't coming home anyway.

"Milly is there anything I can do for ya? I'll stay with you tonight make sure you're ok".

Through sniffles, "I'll be fine, you go home to your Jimmy, I just want to be alone I've so much to think about".

The sunlight beamed in the dusty room, particles falling like glitter highlighted by cigarette smoke. They sat in silence. Mary didn't know what to say, and Milly was numb.

Sean would look after her. Mary was right about that. She'd never be left alone, her father was a brute and deserved everything he got thought Mary. One less drunken beating to take.

The day ended at the dock, the time to act out their plan neared. Sean sauntered behind them with Jimmy.

"You think I should go see her?".

"Yes you should but keep ya mouth shut, do you no good now to confess she'll be a mess".

"God I will, I mean I won't say anything, I'll go over later".

Lovett sat in his office still reeling from the vision on the slab. Didn't bother him another dead Irish man, he had bigger things to think about. Time was running out, and he knew something big was coming. He just didn't know what.

O'Hanlon sat at his desk filing paperwork for this and that. He had lost respect for his superior after Clarke's death. He joined the constabulary to be part of something, to help Ireland, but he could now see why they needed independence though he could never see it happening.

He had his suspicions about Jimmy and his gang, it wouldn't be difficult to find the plan, does he help them and go against the law or does he go against them, those who may change Ireland for the better and put his life on the line?

Lovett was useless. Sure he had cracked a few minor cases but nothing this big. Time was running out.

That evening Sean sat in his rooms thinking about Milly. He desperately wanted to see her, he would try his hardest not to confess, but this might be his only opportunity to finally unite with her, the love of his life. He got up and put his jacket on and left before he changed his mind.

The usually short walk felt like it took longer and he was terrified.

He would either get everything he ever wanted or lose it all. He

loved her more than anything in the world, and no amount of sexual

conquests came close to his Milly.

He knocked on the door and waited. He heard shuffling and the door

unlocking, and a tired-looking Milly opened the door.

"Sean!". She was surprised to see him.

"Can I come in, I heard what happened".

"Sure, can I get you a tea?".

"No, I'm fine. I'm so sorry Milly".

"You're sorry? It seems everyone's sorry today" she resigned.

"I bought over a bottle thought we could drink and talk".

She looked over at the golden liquid. She wasn't much of a drinker

after watching how her father was affected by it. Tonight one

wouldn't hurt.

She got two chipped cups from the kitchen and Sean poured. They

sat in silence, looking at the fire, dancing in the soft light. Milly

stared.

"Have they said how it happened?".

"No, not yet. If I know my dad he probably got drunk and fell in knowing him, stupid drunk bastard", she sipped.

Sean looked at his feet, stifling all the voices in his head to confess.

"What will ya do now?".

"Do?".

"Yeah, you won't be able to afford this place on ya own".

"I have family up north I can go to".

Sean's heart sank.

"Or ya could live with me". Milly slowly turned her head to him.

"You're very sweet, Sean, but what would the neighbours think?".

"Who cares what they think, they're probably already talking about ya, you know what they're like, we don't even have to stay here we can go up north together me and you, start a life".

"That's a fanciful idea, Sean, what about Mary and Jimmy and work, we've no money Sean, thanks but I can't".

"Will ya least have a think about it, we're good together Milly, let's move forward I love you" he implored.

"Sean, you must be drunk, I love you too, but this isn't the right time. I have too much to think about. I think you should go, it's been a long day, and I'm exhausted".

Downhearted Sean stood and went to the door. She opened it and kissed him on the cheek. She did love him, but she was right, this wasn't the time and moving in with her boyfriend at this point would be gossip fuel.

She shut the door and went to bed. Sean stood on the empty street alone. The best thing he could do was be there for her; she knew how he felt. It's up to her.

Chapter 42

Brown walked into Lovett's office papers in hand. For a pathologist who dealt with death on a daily basis, he was a chipper fellow.

"Lovett my man, I have the answer to our riddle", he beamed as he poured himself a drink.

"Oh good please sit".

"Our man drowned, high alcohol content, fell in the water and drowned, poor soul. There was an abrasion on his head, so I'm thinking he stumbled hit his head and in he went to the icy depths" he said smiling.

"How can you smile man what's wrong with you?" laughed Lovett.

"In my line of work it's best to smile, everyone who comes to me is a new puzzle, this one was easy, when are you going to send me something difficult" he laughed. He was jovial and red-faced as he knocked the whiskey back.

"I'll let Ms McCaffrey know. Say, definitely died by drowning, no foul play at all?".

"No, none, why?".

"She hangs out with someone we're watching, and he gave her a proper beating recently, wouldn't surprise me if he was taken out. There's no way to determine any other cause of death?".

"I've checked everything, unable to see bruises due to the composition of the body, it's possible he had a fight and fell in, possible but not definite, it's also possible that he passed out on the docks and rolled in, but not definite, what is definite is he drowned and had a high alcohol level. Ergo he drowned. The poor fool was so inebriated he wouldn't have even suffered, my, these are in-depth questions you ask so early in the morning, you're a better Chief Inspector than you are a pathologist" he laughed.

Lovett shouted for O'Hanlon.

"Best be off, got a few more waiting for me downstairs".

O'Hanlon walked in.

"Sir?".

"Come on we have to go see Milly give her the good news".

"Good news sir?".

"Yes, her father, drunk and drowned".

"Well, at least that something".

They walked out of the station and got in the car and drove through the cobbled streets. They sat at the crossroads, Speakers Corner in the distance still listening to the speeches of a free Ireland against Home Rule.

"Look at those idiots, Ireland will never be independent". O'Hanlon sat silently. He was loathsome.

Lovett sighed. As his eyes wandered round in boredom he noticed that the council offices were having a meeting in two weeks, the public was allowed to attend on the future of Ireland, it was to be attended by council leaders, who as usual did not support Ireland as they were in the English pocket.

It suddenly clicked. Lovett knew the answer. Sitting in his car daydreaming, he finally worked it out. The missing guns, the bomb, a big event, it was the meeting they were going to bomb the meeting! His heart raced like a child finally getting that toy he'd always wanted. He'd cracked it. He had to keep calm. One job at a time. Only he knew.

"Are you ok sir?" O Hanlon could feel the excitement.

"Yes, I'm fine come on traffic! Move it!" and the traffic police waved him on. He sped round to Milly's house. He had to do this quickly and thoughtfully. God, why now why today of all days did I just realise it when I have to show compassion he thought.

He pulled up to the house. A car was a rare sight in those days in that area. It was a poor area, and the only vehicles you saw were the police. Curtains twitched as they got out and knocked on the door. O'Hanlon was putting on his hat.

The door opened.

Milly looked at them, and she knew it was bad news.

"Good morning Miss McCaffrey may we come in?", softly spoken words from Lovett, a rarity from him.

She let them in and sat down too nervous to speak.

"Miss McCaffrey we have just had the autopsy, your father drowned. It seems he had a bit too much to drink, hit his head and fell in the water. I'm very sorry".

Tears streamed down her face.

"Is there anything we can do for you, can we get someone to come sit with you?".

"No nobody, You should go, God, what am I going to do?" she cried.

"I'm very sorry, we have to go, here's my card if you need anything, the death certificate is in there", he lay the papers on the desk. They quietly left the sobbing woman to her own devices.

Sitting in the car, Lovett had to act cool. He started the car and drove away.

"Sir, don't you think we should have stayed longer, got her some help?" asked O Hanlon concerned.

"She didn't want help; she'll be fine. I've got to get back to the offices" Lovett asserted.

"Why sir what's the rush?", O'Hanlon was trying to find out what he knew.

"O'Hanlon, please, I'll explain when we get there!".

O'Hanlon was suspicious; he hadn't seen what had set Lovett off; he would soon though.

Lovett pulled up at the station, and briskly walked to his office.

"Shut the door". Lovett lit a cigarette and sat down, smiling to himself. He knew the answer he had cracked the son of a bitches plan, and only he knew it. He passed the cigarette tin to O'Hanlon, something he never did and offered him a smoke. Does this mean he was his equal?

"Sit down O'Hanlon you make me nervous always s standing around, at ease".

"Ok, so you want to tell me what's happening?".

"O'Hanlon I cracked it, I know what's going to happen, I know where and I know when".

"How sir? I don't."..

"The council meeting, they're going to bomb the council meeting and wipe out the MP's, Jimmy and his team, I have him I finally have him".

"You want me to bring him in sir?" asked the young officer.

"No we can't yet we don't have any definite proof, leave this to me. Go back on duty son, say nothing to no one you hear?".

"Yes, sir".

He left and shut the door, and Lovett sat thinking. He was right he couldn't just send out a team and arrest someone on a hunch. Even he was correct.

He had to be careful and catch them in the act. Finally, Lovett had cracked a big one.

Chapter 43

Milly made her way down to Mary's; she had to see someone she knew, she hammered on the door, and Mary opened it.

"Milly come in what's happened?".

"I'll make tea" beamed Mrs Riordan.

"That's ok I'm fine".

"Well, I'll make one anyway".

Milly sat.

"So?" Mary searching her face for answers.

"The police came today. He drowned, my dad hit his head when he was drunk and fell in the water and drowned".

"Oh Milly love, I'm so sorry," said Mary wrapping her arms around her tearful friend.

Milly collapsed in her arms tears and sobs jerking her body.

"What am I gonna do? I'll get kicked out".

"You won't. You can live here with us; there's loads of room isn't there, Ma?".

"Of course Milly we won't see ya on the streets".

"Didn't Sean come and see ya?".

"Yeah he wants me to live wi him but the neighbours".

"Oh to hell with the neighbours".

"Mary!" scolded Ma.

"Sorry, Ma but still it's nothing to do with them, he's a lovely guy. I think you should".

"If you need help with the funeral we can have it here if you like," said Ma trying to be sympathetic, she also didn't like Milly's father, and you shouldn't wish ill on the dead, but in this case, she hoped it was hot where he was.

They drank tea and calmed down.

"Milly, you want your tea here?".

"No thanks I'm gonna go home I have to speak to the church and organise the funeral. So much to do".

"You're not alone there. We'll help".

"I appreciate it thank you so much". Milly got up and hugged them both and left.

As she was walking Jimmy and Sean saw her, they were returning home.

"Hey Milly" shouted Jimmy "hold up" and they sprinted to her.

"Hi".

"Have you heard anything about your Da, what happened?" Jimmy asked, Sean silent.

"The police came round this morning, he hit his head when he was drunk and fell in the water, drowned. I'm after going to organise the funeral. I just seen your Mary congratulations on your engagement".

"Thanks yeah next year we hope, listen if you need anything, I'm sorry what happened to your Da, listen I gotta go, Sean, will ya walk her home?".

"Oh no, it's not necessary. It's not far".

"I'll walk with ya it's nice out," said Sean, and they went their separate ways.

The couple didn't speak much as they walked; it was like they had run out of words.

Sean, though glad they got away with murder, still felt the pain of guilt inside. They got to the door and Milly turned.

"Thanks for walking me home".

"It's no problem. You want to come out tonight, go for a drink, take your mind off things?".

Milly looked down as he held her hand. Red knuckles. Cracked. Bruised. Unusual as it's not the place you get injuries unless you been in a fight. She looked up at him and declined, why had this bothered her so much, Sean wasn't one to get in fights.

"Sean I have to go".

She snatched her hand back and shut the door. Thoughts were racing. Fighting with each other. Surely not. Sean was angry about what her father had done, but he wouldn't have done anything about it, it was Sean, quiet, meek, wouldn't hurt a fly. Still, the thought wouldn't leave her mind.

Chapter 44

Lovett sat staring out the window forming a plan. He had to be smart once word that got out could lead to his plan being foiled and the target changing.

But, word had got out. O'Hanlon knew. He was trusted, and so it was easy to hide his loyalties. Would O'Hanlon go against the constabulary or would he become an informer?

Jimmy and his team sat at the table, working out the plan.

"The meeting is at 11 am, we have to act quickly. Davey, you place the bomb in the reception,

wear your Sunday best and carry it in a bag, you'll tell them you're waiting for someone and take a seat and then wait, leave the bag under the seat and walk out. Colin, me and you two will wait on the corner. When everyone comes running out, we take them out. There'll be chaos so no one will see us. No Nose you keep a lookout for the police, any trouble walk passed us, we all go separate ways got it?".

The lads through hazy cigarette smoke nodded.

"I won't lie to ya lads, we probably won't make it back, if any of you do make it back, no contact, they don't know us, but we know them, get away from here as soon as you can. When it's died down you can come back, the lads in Birmingham know about the plan, they will hide you".

"What about Mary?" asked Colin.

"What about Mary?" replied Jimmy.

"Well if you're saying we need to leave or that we mightn't come back, you're taking a risk to leave Mary".

"The less she knows, the better, I'm not planning on dying or leaving, none of us are, it's just in case".

"That Lovett, we gonna get him after what he did to Clarke?".

"Leave him to me, the bastards got it coming", Jimmy scowled.

"That copper, you think he help us?",

"A copper help us? I wouldn't bank on it. He seems like a top fella. We keep an eye on him. He might be useful in time".

They smoked and drank and drew their plans, not knowing if they would come back or not.

Milly sat by the fireside, she could not get the image of Sean's knuckles from her mind, he had been skittish around her which was nothing new, but there was something behind his eyes that she could tell there was something. Not her Sean though, he was kind and gentle with her, sure he hated her father, but he had many enemies, she didn't believe that her father merely drowned, he drank God knows he drank, but he always made it home, what was he doing by the docks anyway?

There were too many secrets in Belfast. Her suspicions kept her awake. She decided to see Lovett; after all, he did say if she needed anything to call on him.

Chapter 45

The deadline approached quicker with every hour, and Lovett still hadn't worked out his plan.

He called a meeting with Superintendant Green to discuss his suspicions and plan. This was the biggest thing he had come across, and they had to be smart.

"Superintendant," said Lovett stood to attention.

"Chief".

Green sat at the table and mulled over the information. He sighed quietly thinking. He never had any faith in Lovett, a pompous buffoon who couldn't solve a crossword let alone a case of this magnitude. He was surprised and a little jealous.

"Have we got any intel from the informers?".

"Yes, we were told guns were coming into the city, I interviewed Jimmy Mahon, but it came up with nothing, he's a clever one that".

"For you maybe. And you're sure he's in on it?".

"Yes, our informer confirmed".

"Where is this informer, bring them in".

Lovett looked down. He had sent Briona away.

"That won't be possible sir, she left town some time ago, they know who she is, and they put a hit on her, so she left".

"You let her leave?".

"I didn't have much of a choice sir she wasn't that much use after she told us what she saw".

"What did she see?".

"The Dockers Rest, the landlord hid guns there, we checked it out, but it was cold, the landlord looked frightful like someone had got to him, he won't talk. Sir with all due respect we need to move quickly, that meeting needs insiders, our insiders to keep watch, we need the surrounding areas watched and Jimmy too".

"I'll tell you what's needed thank you very much, it's only by happenstance that you got this far Lovett, if it were up to me you'd be on the beat with the lack of work you do around here, you got nothing from Clarke at all and ended up with a body that I had to clear up and got us into deeper discord with the natives when we're trying to get them on our side, you have caused this rumpus, and once again I have to clear it up".

"Sir," said Lovett quietly like a schoolboy.

Green looked in the distance, Lovett was right, but he'd never let on.

"We don't have that much manpower. We'll get a man in the meeting and place sentries on the roof to look out. Their security will check bags and do a sweep and advise them to be watchful. The meeting is at 11, you say?".

"Yes, sir".

"Seems our gang are night owls, the hotel across the road, I'll set a man inside to watch for any activity and get him to radio in anything".

"What shall I do sir?".

"Do what you always do, nothing. You'll stay here and we'll let you know if we need you".

"Sir, this is my case!".

"And you've taken long enough to get here, and you ask for my assistance to form even the most basic of plans as you lack both the brains and the intelligence to form one yourself, my God man how you managed to worm your way in my station with nothing to show for it, look at this office, seems more like a bar than a place of order! You will stay here, and you will be on call should we need you. I don't want to hear another word, and you will keep your mouth shut, is that clear?!".

"Sir". Green stood and left. Lovett was fuming inside. For his valiant efforts had got results, but his reputation for being slow and ineffectual had bettered him. Stay here my arse, he thought.

He called O'Hanlon in who had been listening intently. His face belied his thoughts. Though he did not like Lovett or his methods, he had felt pity for him after the rebuke.

"O'Hanlon, I suppose you heard?".

"I did sir".

"Go the Rest tonight, have a drink and see if you can hear anything of interest and report to me only, say nothing to anyone but me understand?".

"Yes sir, I see Jimmy and his men in there sir quite often would it not be beneficial to send other men in, I mean they may recognise me".

"They may. It might be a benefit if they do, a stranger they may not talk at all; you have to be careful".

O'Hanlon agreed and walked out. Lovett would not get the glory, but he would get the son of bitch before the day was out.

Chapter 46

Milly made her way to the station. Her suspicions were eating away at her sanity. There was a battle in her mind. It could be a coincidence, or it could mean something, reasoning with herself then going against herself, she had to get some closure she needed to know.

Making her way in, O'Hanlon was at the desk. The noisy drunks and street criminals making their presence known, a tiny woman was not a usual sight.

"Ah Miss McCaffrey, how can I help you today?" he asked jovially.

"Is Mr Lovett in?".

"Chief Inspector Lovett" he corrected.

"Fine, whatever is he in or not?".

"He is, but he's very busy, can I help you at all?".

"No, I really need to see him. It's about my Da",

"Take a seat I'll go check", he left the desk and knocked the closed door. A loud muffled voice called in him, O'Hanlon walked in and a for a few silent minutes Milly watched, she knew he wouldn't help her. His disingenuous offer of help was routine that he didn't ever assume she would take him up on.

He walked out with O'Hanlon and beckoned her in.

"Miss McCaffrey, welcome, please take a seat. I'm very busy, so I only have a few minutes, how are you holding up?".

"Chief Inspector I want to talk about my father's death, you said it was an accident, but I don't think it was".

"Oh?".

"See, why was he at the docks? He never goes there, and he always makes it home".

"That I don't know, Milly, I'm sorry about what happened to you and your father, but it's best not to think about these things, he's in a better place now". Trying to sound both caring and wanting her gone as soon as possible. He didn't have time for a small town drunk.

"A better place!" she said scornfully, "That's it? A better place? I think he was murdered" her anger rising.

There was silence as Lovett looked at her. She was but a little girl in his eyes, meek and frail.

"Murder? By whom".

"I don't know that's your job to find out".

"Miss McCaffrey there is no evidence that he met an untimely end, the pathologist confirmed, he was drunk he fell in he drowned".

"I don't believe it".

"Of course you don't, he was your dad, and you're looking for someone to blame to ease your pain, it's understandable. Forget all about this theory. It's not healthy".

"It's not a theory you need to do your job!".

"I have done my job, don't presume to come in here and tell me I haven't! This matter is closed".

"I think Sean had something to do with it".

"Sean?".

"Sean Cross, I think he and Jimmy Mahon had something to do with it".

Lovett's ears pricked up, "Jimmy Mahon how I am tired of hearing his name, what evidence do you have?".

"Well, nothing really but.".."

"You built this nonsense on nothing really?! Why are you wasting my time with this", He said sternly. Who cares about another drunk Irish he thought, he had no time for this.

"I saw Sean he had bloody knuckles".

"Show me a man who doesn't, could have been from a fight or anything".

"He acts skittish around me".

"That's probably 'cause you're a beautiful young lady, Milly, please I'm very sorry for what happened, and you have my deepest condolences, but I really must get on, just go home and have a nice cup of tea ok, live your life and remember the good times you had with your father".

"Fine, I'll do my own investigation then, and I'll bring him in myself".

"As you wish madam" he sighed. You could never argue with a woman.

Milly left, frustrated and angry, maybe he was right, perhaps he fell in and drowned, but at the back of her mind, the seed of doubt grew and grew.

Chapter 47

Mary sat at home with Ma sewing. They could sit for a while like this, not speaking and enjoy each others company. The engagement had bought a brighter future for them all. It had been a long time since they had good news. Ireland was a ticking bomb and Home Rule the spark.

"Mary, have you two set a date yet?".

 "No, not yet Ma, there's so much to do. I don't know where to start", Mary replied, concentrating on her needle.

"A date would be a good start; then we have to book the church, find you a dress".

"I thought I could just wear yours Ma, be my something old".

"Oh, that would be grand, what would your something blue be?".

 "Ha, that be Da after he's had a few",

the women chuckled.

Mary had butterflies when she thought of Jimmy, but at the back of her mind, she felt unease. He was hiding something from her; she could always tell. His eyes told a different story to one he was telling her and had hoped that it was not criminal. She knew about his past, and she forgave him, every man was a fighter she knew that much.

She wanted Milly to be a bridesmaid; after the death of her father, it would be a welcome break.

"I asked Milly to be my bridesmaid Ma".

"That'll be lovely poor girl, I do feel for her".

"At least that wretch won't be beatin her no more".

"He did like to use his fists that one, I knew the drink would get him one day, I just wish Sean would hurry and marry her, they make a lovely couple".

"Sean asked her to marry him? I'd love to see that, took him long enough to ask her out".

"He's a shy one but a good one, who knows maybe he asks her at the wedding, might inspire him".

"I won't hold me breath".

The fire crackled in the silence, and Mary would miss these times when she left and lived with Jimmy.

Chapter 48

Lovett, Green and O'Hanlon were looking at maps to work out the best location to place the men.

"The town hall needs to be covered on all four sides" pointed Green to a murmur of agreement.

"We'll have two men inside and officers in transit here, here and here, all sides will be covered. Bedford Street and Upper Arthur Street on the corner of Chichester Street, Donegal Place will be blocked off so they won't be able to get through without checks. O'Hanlon, you'll be at Bedford Street on the look out, you see anything you radio in. Got it, lads?".

"Sir" they all echoed in unison.

"Lovett, you will stay here and keep in radio contact should we need you" ordered Green, Lovett had the reputation of being incompetent and was treated like a child, there was nothing he could do about this, he was scorned and was just happy that he had cracked the case even though he would get no recognition. He would be back in Blighty soon enough he thought, away from this place with the idle Irish he so despised.

The maps were put away, and the lads left. He called O'Hanlon.

"Have you found anything yet?".

"No I'm going to the Dockers tonight sir, they're pretty regular in there, won't be too hard to find them".

"Be careful, if they find out we know, then it could blow the whole thing".

"Excellent sir".

O'Hanlon was fighting his inner demons. Would he stay true to the British cause, or would he go against it? He now saw the injustices happening around him, and his loyalties were changing.

His loyal face belied his intentions. It's easy to lie when you are trusted.

Chapter 50

Jimmy and his lads were in for their usual drink, discussing all sorts, his upcoming marriage.

"Jimmy we need to have a stag night for you, celebrate your freedom while you still have it" laughed Sean.

"Stag night! Mary'd kill me if I got too hammered".

"So when's the big day then lad you haven't said".

"Let's get this out the way first, might be a funeral first" he laughed.

"Ah we be ok, if they don't kill ya Mary will".

"Oh to die by a woman's hand".

"Or her thighs" exclaimed Davey, and they all laughed riotously.

It was good to see Sean out, back to his old self. He seems to have forgotten his troubles and moved on. Unaware of the plan, there was an atmosphere brooding, Jimmy always kept him safe.

The warm bar was packed as usual with the hard-working men, dirty from the shipyard and furnaces.

O'Hanlon walked in; Jimmy clocked him. A secret nod beckoned him to the bar.

Jimmy made his way to the bar. No eye contact and speaking low, you never knew who was listening and watching. O'Hanlon spoke. "They know".

Those two words sent shivers down Jimmy's spine. The only other two words in the English language that would bring the same fear were 'I do'.

Jimmy was silent. He knew O'Hanlon was one of them.

"What's their plan?" asked Jimmy.

"The surrounding roads will be cornered off, I will be on Bedford Street, but there will be roadblocks everywhere else. They have a man inside on the day. You need to forget this Jimmy they want your blood".

"I can't forget it. If we die, we die".

"I'll keep a lookout for you. There'll be two unmarked vans on Bedford and Wellington, Lovett won't be there, he's on the radio at the station".

Jimmy sat listening, Making mental notes. He had to change the plan. He grabbed his beers and walked back to the table. Silent.

"What's the matter with you?" asked Colin.

"Nothing lads, drink up".

Jimmy sat, staring at his now empty pint glass. He had to tell them what he heard.

"Sure what's the matter Jimmy?" asked Sean.

"Sean you don't need to know".

"Come on I'm ya best mate let me know already".

Eyes stared at Jimmy. So far, Sean knew nothing. He wasn't a loose cannon, but the less he knew, the safer he was. Still, Jimmy had to come clean.

"Sean, lads, we need to go drink up".

They exited the pub and made their way to Sailor-town, Sean in tow.

"Sean are ya going home?" asked Davey, No Nose watching as usual.

"I hadn't planned on it, what's all the secrecy you're making me feel like an eejit".

The group stopped and looked at their leader.

"Sean, I love you like a brother you know that right" said Jimmy his hands on his shoulders.

"Of course I do". Jimmy leaned in and whispered in his ear the plan and waited for a reaction.

Sean looked at him, incredulously.

"You can't be serious!". Sean looked like a frightened child. Jimmy was the only family he had.

Jimmy nodded as did the others. He trusted Sean not to say anything.

"But you'll get killed you know what they do to people like you; you can't be thinking about Mary".

"I am thinking about Mary, I'm thinking of all of Ireland".

"What use will you be if you're dead?".

"I'm not planning on dying now, are you with us or against us?" demanded Jimmy. Eyes locked on him for any sign of weakness.

"Jimmy, I'm with you all the way, but there has to be another way, all this fighting, it's getting us no where".

"They killed Clarke Sean they need to pay, how many more Irish men need to die for freedom that the British have by birth?".

"I don't know, but this isn't the way! You're mad!".

"I am mad, I'm furious, I can't lie down and take it any more something needs to be done, I won't sit down and be relegated any more. Come on, you're one of us now".

"One of you?" Sean asked rhetorically.

"All you have to do is keep your mouth shut, do ya hear".

"Yes I hear". Keeping his mouth shut was something he had recently had experience in.

The lads walked to the house. The plan needed to change.

They walked in. Sean got a look. They were suspicious of him.

Would Sean foil the plan or would his loyalties to Jimmy come through? They had to trust him. They had no choice.

"They know". Said Jimmy. The group all looked at each other.

"Who knows?" asked Colin.

"O'Hanlon told me, he told me where they are going to be, and there'll be roadblocks. He's going to help us, but we need to change the plan".

"You trust a copper?" asked Colin.

"I told you, he's one of us".

They all looked at each other. Too many people knew, and the risks were increasing.

"So what do we do now?" asked Davey.

"We stick to the plan, but we move in quicker. The meeting is at 11 am right, they'll be there before us, but if we get in before them, you plant that bomb the day before, you hock a van and park it at the vantage point on Linenhall so they won't have a chance to park it too near, place another bomb in there and one on the corner of Bedford. They won't have set the roadblocks up until the next day, time them all to go off at 11.10 am then when they run out we shoot. Davey, Colin, you think you can do this?".

"Sure don't see why not".

"You two, you can have them ready by then?".

"Not a problem we have all the stuff here. What about him?" pointing at Sean.

"Don't worry about him, he's the lookout. Sean, you walk the street you see anything you cross at Donegal square, and we'll know something's up".

Sean nodded. It was a plan he didn't want to be part of, but now he had no choice and Jimmy would never let anything happen to him.

"Where are you going to be?".

"Lovett is holed up at the station, I'm going to wait for him to go out and then I'm gonna pop him".

"At the station? Don't you think it's risky?".

"He thinks he's safe there, as long as he thinks I'm with you he won't know I'm right under his nose".

The meeting ended, and they all went their own way.

Sean was now an accessory and sworn to secrecy. Even if he did warn the police, which he wouldn't, they'd never believe that he had nothing to do with it, all Irish are criminals in their eyes.

Chapter 51

Milly's paranoia grew. She made her way to Mary's house to discuss her suspicions. Like Jimmy, Mary was level headed and would give her the answers she needed.

"Ah Milly, I'm glad you're here".

"I want to ask you something " said Milly.

"Oh?".

"I think Sean had something to do with me dads death".

"How so? I thought your dad rest his soul drowned?".

"That's what they say, but he always made his way home and why was he at the docks anyway?".

"That I don't know, maybe he went the wrong way and just fell in, he was a drunk mind".

"Sean has marks on his knuckles".

"And? Maybe it's from the docks they have some terrible injuries there".

"That's what Lovett said, but he's been acting really strange lately like he knows something".

"Sean's acts weird in front of you because he loves ya and I wouldn't worry about the knuckles, he may have had a fight, but I doubt he would do anything like that, here have a cuppa settle your mind girl, Sean's a good lad".

"It's right at the back of my mind. You think I should ask him?".

"Ask him if he killed ya Da, sure what you expect him to say yes I did it, what if he didn't do it and you ask him and ruin everything?".

"I'd rather know the truth".

"I wouldn't ask him it'd do no good if you were wrong".

"And what if I'm right?".

"If you're right, what will you do with the information?".

"Tell Lovett".

"Tell Lovett? Do you want to see Sean hang? Your dad was a drunk, I'm sorry, but he was, and he beat you unmerciful, if he did meet an untimely death at someone's hands it's probably cause he deserved it. Milly you have been given a chance at life, a good life, I doubt Sean would do it but if he did he did because he loves you so".

"He did have a lot of enemies, but I can't get it out me head or sleep thinking about it, I can't have a life with Sean unless I know the truth".

"Jimmy always says you shouldn't ask questions you don't want the answer to" Mary sighed, Jimmy was right. It as a no-win situation.

"How is your Jimmy? I haven't seen him in a while".

"He's working, constant up there, that ship is taking forever, oh it'll be grand when she's done".

"That she will. Do you trust Jimmy?" asked Milly.

"Oh what a question of course I do, I wouldn't marry him otherwise, why do you ask?".

"I just, him and Sean they're like brothers, what if he knows what happened to Da?".

"If Jimmy knew anything I'd know, I can read him like a book. If it bothers you that much go ask Sean, but think about it first, you don't want to start anything you can't finish".

Milly nodded slowly, her mind racing as she drank her tea. Mary was right. She had to confront him. Good or bad news, she had to free her mind.

Milly walked home and thought about meeting Sean. She diverted to his house and knocked on the door. Her hand trembling. She was more scared of his answer than her father beating her. The locks turned and the door opened to his blue eyes glistening in the sun.

"Milly what a nice surprise come in, can I get you anything?" he turned to the living room. With his back turned Milly just blurted it out.

"Did you kill my father?". Sean stood not facing her. Silence.

Milly's heart racing. She repeated.

"Milly I.".

"Why Sean why!" tears welling up, her hands coming to her face wishing this was a bad dream.

"Milly it was an accident!" Sean declared, holding her arms as she tried to hit him.

"An accident? Why Sean, what did he do?!"

"Milly he beat ya, he was going to take you away from me, I did it out of love, Milly please you have to forgive me!" he cried.

"Sean Oh my God, you killed him, you killed him!" and she collapsed, crying in his arms as he rocked her.

"I did it out of love".

"Love sure what would you know about love, are you the judge and jury now!" she stood up and pushed him off.

"I can't believe you, Sean!" tears streaming down her face.

"Please, please, I wanted to tell you I did, but Jimmy said not to".

"Jimmy knows?".

"Jimmy was there, but he had nothing to do with it, it was me, he was drunk, and he saw me and started shouting that he was hauling you away and that we'd never see each other again and I lost it, we had a fight and fell, I didn't know what to do so we rolled him into the Lagan, Milly I did it for you".

Milly was silent, heavily breathing in shock, Jimmy knew.

"I have to get out of here, don't touch me". Milly ran home hysterical. Jimmy knew. Mary didn't.

Would she tell Mary and ruin her life or keep it to herself and ruin only her own? The clarity she sought only made things worse. Mary was right. You should ask questions you don't want the answer to.

Chapter 52

The day had arrived. Plans were set. Jimmy made his way to Mary's

house. He didn't know if he would be back.

"Good morning Jimmy, you're here awful early".

"I had to see you, Mary, we need to talk".

"Sounds serious".

"Mary I love you

more than anything in the whole world".

"I know that you came here at this hour to tell me that? You old

softy" she said, smiling.

"Mary, I'm an Irish man, and I have to do something today that I

might not be back from, but you have to know I love you".

"Jimmy you're scaring me, what's going on? Is this to do with

Milly?".

"Milly?" he frowned.

"Yeah she came here asking if you and Sean had anything to do with

her Dads death I told her she was being silly".

"No it's nothing to do with that".

"So you did have something to do with it?".

"Mary can you just let me finish" frustration in his voice as she interrupted him.

"Ok sorry carry on".

"Look, the police might show up at some point, but you don't know anything ok".

"That's right I don't know anything, Jimmy whatever it is, and I think it's pretty bad of you saying that you might not be back, please don't do it think of me, us, our future".

"I am thinking of you and our future". He held her tight, looking into her eyes.

"Our future is here Jimmy, there's no future unless you're in it".
Mary was welling up.

"I have to go".

"Jimmy wait please, you don't, stay here with me whatever it is, if you leave that door I won't be here when you get back" trying to make him stay.

"Mary love I have to go. I will be back. I just need you to trust me".

"Jimmy I love you, stay please" she screamed, she knew he wouldn't be back, and she would never see him again, she implored him to stay, held on to him tightly.

He kissed her hard and walked out the door leaving poor Mary.

She was panicking inside. Her Ma walked in, and Mary was pacing.

"Ma, I think Jimmy's in trouble!".

"Why love what's up" she replied worriedly.

"He just left he said if any police come around to say nothing".

"Nothing about what?" asked Ma.

"I don't know, but he said he might not be back and that he loves me, I don't know what he's planning, but I begged him to stay what do I do? Ma I'm scared" Mary cried into her mother's arms.

"Now now, we don't know anything for sure, calm down it's probably just men's business". Her grown-up daughter was always her little girl no matter what, and she always had a hanky up her sleeve for tears and sniffles.

"Where's Da? He'd know what to do".

"Ya Da went out this morning for his paper he be back soon".

"I'm going out to find him. I can't think", and Mary stood frantically looking for her shawl.

"I'll put the kettle on for when you get back, don't worry Mary I'm sure it's nothing".

Mary wrapped her shawl and ran through the streets, crowds of people were making their way to the centre, a busy Saturday as usual. Mary didn't see her father, but she saw Jimmy but lost him in the crowd.

She saw his friends. Her eyes followed them.

She saw Davey walking out and No Nose reading the paper and Sean standing on the corner desperately trying to be ignored. Colin was in a van looking over his paper.

Mary waited to see what was happening. She looked over and saw that the town hall was having a meeting, and it all clicked. Her heart sank; this is what Jimmy meant. He may not come back as he might die or go to jail.

What could she do but watch and wait.

But where was Jimmy?

Why had he gone the other way, what was that way? She decided to walk along and see if she could work it out. It didn't take long. Down the street where she saw him go, she saw the station. Why would he go to the station? He wouldn't be stupid enough to go there, surely? She looked around and saw him. She stayed hidden to see what his move was.

Jimmy sat waiting. Contemplating. His Mary was his life, but this was important. It was his chance to make a difference.

Something unpredictable happened. Milly had walked into the station. Jimmy watched with horror. What was she doing? Why was she here? Even Mary was perturbed by this move. Had she confronted Sean? Minutes felt like hours. Could Mary have one last try at changing Jimmy's mind, he could still walk away from it no one would blame him. Her mind raced. She had to act quickly. She would open her mouth and shout, but no sound came, and her legs wouldn't move.

Lovett came out with Milly holding her arm. They couldn't hear what she was saying, but from his body language it was not good, Lovett threw her out on the street and Milly walked away, Lovett perused the street and Jimmy looked up. He grabbed his gun this was his moment. It was now or never. He got out the van and Lovett saw him. He turned to run back in, but it was too late.

"For Clarke!" yelled Jimmy as he fired shots at Lovett. Lovett fell on the steps as Jimmy approached him. People stood watching, Mary wide-eyed.

Jimmy stood over him. Lovett gurgled his breath as the blood seeped away.

"This is for Clarke" scorned Jimmy staring down at him.

"You won't get away Jimmy we're watching you" Lovett said weakly.

Jimmy shot him in the face and ran.

He didn't see Mary watching, frozen. Jimmy signed his own death warrant. She turned and leaned up the wall, her heart beating rapidly. What could she do now?

BANG!!! The sky echoed. It had begun.

Chapter 52

Bricks and rubble rained from the sky. Shots were taken. Men's voices muffled in the confusion. Mary ran to the commotion. Davey and Colin were taking cover behind the van, British soldiers and police converging like a disturbed ant farm, radios blaring for back up.

Men running from the building trying to get through the smoke. Bystanders were screaming, and mothers were running with their babies, bodies lying in the street.

Jimmy was running to Colin, Sean frozen on the spot. A fighter he was not. Jimmy beckoned him to come, but he couldn't. He backed off and ran for his life. Jimmy knew he would run. He wasn't a coward and Jimmy wouldn't blame him.

Milly was coming too. Her fathers gun in hand. She ran to the commotion and saw Sean. He ran towards her to protect her, to get her away.

"Milly you can't be here", and he grabbed her to take her home.

"I told the police what you did, Sean but they wouldn't help me, you killed my father, Sean!".

"Milly not now!" and he tried to pull her away. He felt a hard object pressing against his stomach.

BANG! Sean bent over double. Fell to the floor.

"Milly" he murmured.

"I'm sorry Sean". Milly looked at him as he loosed his grip on her and fell to the floor, grabbing his stomach in agony, his blue eyes fading, he held out a hand for her. She backed away mouthing her sorry's.

Milly ran through the streets. Jimmy saw Sean lying on the ground. He got up and ran to him and help him.

"Sean! Oh God Sean stay with me I get you out of here".

"It's too late Jimmy". His words were difficult to say.

Jimmy tears in his eyes; there was nothing he could do.

"The bastards" Jimmy retorted.

"It was Milly" whispered Sean.

"What?".

"It was Milly".

Jimmy had tears forming in his eyes.

Sean's head lulled, and he was gone. Jimmy wiped Sean's forehead, his brother in arms was gone.

Oh God, he thought. He laid him down and ran back.

A stray bullet with his name, destined for him hit him in the leg. He was down. He crawled through the chaos to the van, another bullet. He wasn't getting up.

A police officer approached him and finished the job. His grave the streets of Belfast.

Mary ran over to him, lain on his body, screaming, "Not my Jimmy". The officer tried to pull her away, but she wouldn't move. He kicked her and grabbed her shoulder, but there she stayed.

"I'm warning you!" he ordered.

"Fuck off! My Jimmy, my Jimmy" she cried.

The officer shot her too. His coldness was frightening. Another Irishman dead.

Colin and Davey were under fire, No Nose was nowhere. He had made a getaway. The bomb makers were gone. They would fight another day.

Milly ran through the streets. Tears at what she had done.

She stopped at the docks where her father has been taken down. She looked out. The sea was rough. The clouds were coming in. The distant sirens and shouts echoed in the wind.

"I did it for you Da", she put the gun to her head and pulled the trigger.

Her body fell over the sea, and she went to the icy depths.

Chapter 53

Green and his men were radioing Lovett for back up in the chaos.

"Where is the fool, Lovett come in" Green screamed into the radio.

"Sir you want me to go get him?" asked O'Hanlon.

"No I'll deal with him later" Green replied angrily.

The chaos wore down, and Colin and Davey walked out with their

hands up. It was a losing battle, one way or the other they would be

at death's door pretty soon.

The group had lost the battle but, caused enough mayhem to show

they were not taking Home Rule or the British lying down.

They met the hang man's noose at Crumlin.

Ireland would never be free of tyranny, but she would not go down

easily.

Unlike Titanic.

Printed in Great Britain
by Amazon